克里斯托夫・歐克姆瓦 著
Poemed by Christopher Okemwa

羅得彰 譯
Translated by Te-chang Mike Lo

蜂蜜酒上
的暮光

漢 英 雙 語 詩 集

CHRISTOPHER OKEMWA:
Selected Poems

目次

自然與美色

風

我聽到你唱歌，向
四面八方颼颼哮鳴
搖著並吹掉廢棄小屋
的茅草屋頂

擠過茂密的灌木叢
森林，新砍伐的樹籬
一路狂飆，在一片有激烈爭吵的
黑暗林間空地扎根

你舉起五彩紙屑、花綵和舊
麻袋，將它們撒在天空中
然後你抱怨和哭泣時
從線上挑選輕便的衣服

將它們扔在柏油路上
遠處的小路、灌木叢和田野

毛茸茸的旗幟飄揚著，呼呼作響，
絨毛和毛皮旋飛上升

你透過牆上吱吱作響的開窗
進入我們的臥室
破壞蚊帳和窗戶
你淘氣地搖擺徘徊

弄皺毛毯和床單，
微移床頭櫃上的陶器
顫抖著、發出嗚嗚聲
並以輕柔的可跳舞高音離開房間

有時你悄悄地飄過，
吞下你的憤怒和驕傲
傾聽著，有人可能認為你有
跌倒、暈倒並死去

9

卻突然外面的葉子
點頭、飄飄和坐立不安
因此意識到你還活著，
吹著動人的曲子

強風中，你總是興致勃勃地
回來，在樹叢中發牢騷
潺潺穿過茂密的灌木籬笆；
一個刮葫，抱怨和隆隆發聲

沒來由，留下破碎
樹枝、散落的樹枝和樹葉
講述你的威力，
一種強大的憤怒，一種炫耀的驕傲的憤怒

奇妙的夜晚

有時當我看夜景時，我會感到很驚訝
星星落在黑暗碗形天空的方式
月亮披著閃亮的銀白色條紋
像間諜一樣躲在綿羊雲朵後面偷看

我看著這張黑紙──一團黑暗
我發現這是一個讓我充滿畏懼和恐怖的謎
從它的黑暗中空空間，它的無盡空虛之海
可以輕易地生出惡魔、小魔鬼或巨型食人魔

或者只是一些乖戾、惡毒和邪惡的東西
可以吞噬我、消耗或帶走我的靈魂
所以我總是透過窗戶偷看以確保沒有這樣的惡魔
在其可怕的無定形徘徊中湧進房間

我很難想像夜晚會怎樣：
不祥的寂靜在每個迷你空間裡守夜

遮蔽雙眼的不透明黑色使眼睛看不見
它的黑色皮毛和灰色油漆構成了錯綜複雜的迷宮

夜如翻騰的海，波濤洶湧的海洋
我總是看到它從牆上的窗戶溢出
以它狂暴的動作把我淹沒在我的臥室裡
讓我窒息哽咽，我的靈魂死去

我不敢想像有人出於惡意
可能某晚會有使用宇宙的巨型時鐘之權
然後不讓那小玩意不動，以反抗神明的創物
我們要永遠生活在黑暗中嗎？——地獄對我們來說將是怎
樣的體驗！

蜂蜜酒上的暮光

蜂蜜酒裡寂靜無聲，深沉而甜美
散發著菊花蔓延的香氣
柔和的暮光在鬱鬱蔥蔥的綠地上發酵

和平與滿足下垂蓋著灌木叢
與木柵欄和要成熟的番石榴樹
籠罩在橙色夕陽的光環和美麗中

在成長的玉米和穄子
親吻厚外套，擁抱溫暖的休閒褲
當我拖著腳走過時高粱友善行禮

點狀大小的禿鷹裝飾水洗藍色蒼穹
懶洋洋地飄浮在空中；天空晴朗
月亮現在升起來了，蒼白的，但幾乎是圓的。

田園詩情

走過灌木鋪成的角落

看到尷尬的景象：

一個鄉下怪老人，他的下巴和他的環境一樣茂密

蹲在淺灌木叢中

眼神狂野，上大號；他的臉

是一首民謠，淋漓盡致地體現

我們的童年但已消散的地方

走得更遠些，一個光溜溜的

小屁孩會噗嗤聲地跨過泥濘道路

歷史的鐘擺

在生殖神龕前擺搖

訴說昔時的我們

在薄暮時的啤酒派對相遇衣冠不整

頑固的母親，他們的臀部被鬆散

月經染色的萊索斯[*1]覆蓋

聽他們攙雜的談話

影射、幽默和笑聲

在劍麻墊上度過你的夜晚，在早上
醒來後頭痛揮之不去
烏鴉、咩咩聲和低沉的聲音充斥著清晨的空氣
當你離開村莊時
你會需要一雙厚靴子
涉過重重糞堆的小路。

*1 萊索斯（Lesos）：東非產的彩色棉布。

鑼

我童年更響亮的鈴聲
它的回聲衝進來，更快
每晚在我夢裡
追上我

自行車、驢車
農民的敞篷貨車
在這條鵝卵石路上跑來跑去
留下塵跡

我坐在這裡，在這蟻丘上
在趕集日
數人、驢子
那時我是一個獨來獨往的人
螳螂就是我的泰迪熊。

地球

扁球體
或像尺一樣扁平
或像球一樣圓
沒關係
無論是山脊、斜坡還是小丘
它的頭皮變形
或者山谷，山谷
在它無定形的皮膚上留下凹痕
沒關係
我的是一個標準空間
一個 6 英尺長乘 6 英尺深的矩形世界
將我的靈魂包裹其中
用最閃耀的色彩
紅花和紅絲帶
真的沒關係
扁球體
或像尺一樣扁平

或像球一樣圓

我的空間很小

一個6乘6的矩形世界。

薄暮

晚上的
顏色
現在正在發酵

等待
融化
成一顆夜球

黑暗
尚未觸及
地面

它是女人的眼睛
宇宙
充滿了唧唧聲、顫音

風輕輕地
在吹
地球，慢慢地，睡著了。

今天早上

我坐在高高的帶露草地上
縫過隨機的想法
生活可以多麼美好
清晨的陽光很妖媚
一個裝飾的婚禮新娘
她在樹後形成挑逗的輪廓
光線刺眼
就像馬賽莫蘭[*1]人的箭
在山丘上潑橙色油漆
將天空染成洗白藍色
只是盯著下面的我
生活可以多麼美好

風輕撫我的肌膚
一簇簇草叢相互彎曲
露水把它們黏在一起
讓它們成為相擁的愛人

蜜蜂盤旋在花朵之上
掠飛開，然後掠飛回來
在花蜜上吮吸和流口水
生活可以多麼美好

*1 東非馬賽族的戰士。

政治與政治家

在謊言的講台上

他糖衣包裹的舌頭

蛇的獠牙

對社會有殺傷力

像聖經中的撒該[*1]

貪圖物質財富

他在誦經台上的姿勢

雙手敲擊講台

一個伊阿古[*2]，一個狡詐的邪惡形象

有權力控制

毀滅，不僅是奧賽羅、羅德利哥、

艾米莉亞、苔絲狄蒙娜[*2]

還有他自己和社會

看他歪斜的眼睛

一片奸詐的葉子在瞳孔中飄動

像示劍的亞比米勒[*3]

野心，就像不安分的酸液

在他的動物心中燃燒

24

該隱的印記^{*4}

在他火熱的額頭上

一隻手拿著一塊麵包

另一手拿著一把雙刃劍

以毀滅靈魂，使人流血

注意，善良的人們

成為約坦^{*5}並參選——投票讓他下台

聽聽他對人群說的話

他甚至不聽自己的話。

（發表於《瘋狂：世界詩歌選集》，WPM-尼泊爾，2022年）

*1 撒該（Zacchaeus）：為聖經新約人物，是耶利哥城的海關監督、稅吏長。當時稅吏被視為依服羅馬帝國的人士而被憎恨。

*2 伊阿古（Iago）、奧賽羅（Othello）、羅德利哥（Rodrigo）、艾米莉亞（Emilia）、苔絲狄蒙娜（Desdemona）：都為莎世比亞四大悲劇奧賽羅中的重要人物。

*3 亞比米勒（Abimelech）：為聖經舊約中一人物，他父親死後，為取代其位置，他到他母親家鄉示劍，爭取人民支持。

*4 該隱（Cain）：為聖經舊約中亞當和夏娃的兒子之一，他殺死了他的
 兄弟亞伯。為聖經中人類的第一次殺人事件，而上帝在他身上留下
 一印記，做為祂懲罰罪的警告。
*5 約坦（Jotham）：古代中東國家南猶大王國的第十一任君主，被認為
 其國最正直偉大的國王。

26

他們與我們同在

小心，警惕，注意
黑暗天使與我們同在
總是在選舉期間出現
開著很耗油
有色，厚胎
法拉利、阿斯頓馬丁
愛快羅密歐、布加迪
勞斯萊斯幻影
像群狼一樣咆哮
渴望選民的鮮血
天空一被直升機點綴！
他們像神一樣飛在我們頭頂
莫尼伯格[*1]先生！莫尼伯格先生！
下面的崇拜者變得瘋狂
他受寵若驚，他覺得自己是一座小山
降下並撒發鈔票
像天上的瑪納[*2]
選民相信他鋪天蓋地的謊言

他的富裕、他偷來的財富
他們在他的財富之海中暢游
被他的虛假承諾窒息
被他的諾言絆倒
我會建造圖書館！
我要在學校裡建教室！
我要讓每家每戶有電！
我會為倒楣的可憐孩子付學費！
小心、警惕、注意
他是一條偽裝的蛇
在綠草中滑行
由狂奔的路西法*3所生
帶著銀色的舌頭
一條致命的尾巴，其尖端有毒
他的太陽穴上長著尖角
爪子，一把雙刃彎刀
小心、警惕並注意。

*1 莫尼伯格（Moneyberg）：若直譯為金山。
*2 瑪納（Manna）：聖經中是古代以色列人出埃及時，上帝賜給他們的
神奇食物。
*3 路西法（Lucifer）：文學中路西法常作為魔鬼的本名。

輯

——— 戰爭與和平 ———

三

戰爭就像……

戰爭是一顆臭雞蛋

爆裂破碎

在我們的外表和面孔之前

爆裂四濺

我們奔跑，窒息

緊緊捏住鼻孔

把我們的淚痕

留在後方

我們必朽的足跡

沉入地下

被血的痕跡塗汙

我們埋葬

我們父母的靈魂和骨頭

並用瓦礫和土壤

掩蓋他們的灰色智慧

我們帶著

我們孩子夢想的灰燼

讓它像風一樣吹走
在柴堆上
我們焚毀這一代人
和我們子孫的靈魂。

（出版於《UKRAINE：A World Anthology of Poems on War》，Christopher Okemwa 編輯，2023年）

你一定要告訴你媽嗎？

——獻給我們社區勇士的詩

戰爭開始時

你一定要告訴你媽媽嗎？

你這膽小鬼

你這狗男孩！

你這懶惰小伙子！

是社區的詛咒

年輕一代的恥辱

你一定要告訴你媽媽嗎？

一定要嗎？

你一定要告訴你媽媽嗎？

當吹響戰號時

整個村子動起來

婦女們收集箭並排列長矛

男人們把赭石、黏土和煙灰塗上皮膚

你一定要流連忘返嗎？

你一定要懶洋洋地站著猶豫不決嗎？

一定要嗎？

一定要茫然看視嗎？

你一定要把頭轉回看你媽媽嗎？

你是哪種人？

誰把你生在她肚子裡？

你吸了誰的奶？

誰把你養在她懷裡？

哪把刀劃破了你的包皮？

你這狗男孩！

你個膽小鬼！

一定要嗎？

你一定要告訴你媽媽嗎？

當戰鼓被敲響時

戰士們為死亡和生命排隊

敵人潛伏在尼揚維塔森林[1]後面

該不該回頭去找媽媽？

你該不該？
你應該徵求你母親的忠告嗎？
哦，膽小鬼中的膽小鬼
哦，詛咒中的詛咒
你該不該找你媽媽嗎？
你該不該？
你該不該找你媽媽嗎？

當其他小伙子不在時
鼓聲回盪在村莊的每一個角落
舞者在漫喀山脊上搖晃地面
母牛吼叫
山羊咩咩叫
田野裡充滿了泣聲
戰歌衝破的河岸
和那些含沙射影的人
你一定要不明白我們人民的寓言故事嗎？

你一定要看起來很愚蠢嗎？

你一定要落後嗎？

你一定要在小屋裡烘暖你的埃格塞納[*2]嗎？

哦，膽小鬼中的膽小鬼！

哦，詛咒的詛咒！

你該不該落後嗎？

你該不該告訴你媽媽嗎？

（發表於《Culture & Identity，Vol.1 WORLD》，Robin Barratt
編選，THE POET出版，ISBN：9798414877431，2022）

[*1] 尼揚維塔森林（Nyangweta Forest）：為肯亞西部一座森林。
[*2] 埃格塞納（Egesena），肯尼亞 Abagusii 社區所用的一塊傳統布料，繫
　　在腰部以遮蓋私處的前部。

烏克蘭

子彈和炸彈
像雷雨一樣在烏克蘭隆隆作響
我們的祖先在墳墓裡翻身
哀號，他們的眼淚
洪水填滿第聶伯河[*1]

清晨的陽光
照亮致命幽靈的陰影
地平線是紅色的
英雄鮮血染紅天際
在霍韋爾拉山[*2]和緬丘爾山[*2]上空
喀爾巴阡山脈[*2]的鳥類音樂
在原始毛櫸森林中緩緩消失

夜晚的星星
揭開子彈之火
風之歌為烏克蘭呻吟

在它有翅膀的嘴唇上，它承載著
遠方敵人的秘密

花朵
像子彈一樣跳出
隕石像炸彈一樣從天而降
灰燼、煙霧、岩石和灰塵
合併埋葬死者。

（出版於《UKRAINE: A World Anthology of Poems on War》，
Christopher Okemwa 編輯，2023年）

*1 第聶伯河（Dnieper / Dnipro River）：為歐洲第四長的河流，發源於
　俄羅斯首都莫斯科以西，流經白俄羅斯和烏克蘭，出海口為黑海。
*2 霍韋爾拉山（Hoverla）、緬丘爾山（Brebenskul）、喀爾巴阡山脈
　（Uholka-ShyrokyiLuh）：皆為烏克蘭境內的山。

老禿鷹

寬闊的翅膀
廣闊的圓形尾巴
飄浮在上升氣流上
在基輔上方環繞
在高高的天空中
此存在有諷刺意味嗎？
它象徵著重生嗎？
那麼，我們是不是要
在風中放飛自我
和禿鷹一起飛？

他們的鼻孔張開
他們聞到牛糞
蚱蜢、死蛇
他們張開彎曲的喙
他們看到小蟲子
死臭鼬和小雞

他們猛撲過去
榴彈砲、反坦克手榴彈的噪音
炸彈的煙霧，火箭的灰塵
下面傳來哀號和尖叫聲

吃夠了屍體後
塞飽
它們飛不起來
一部分失去了生命
哦，莫斯科
反芻
以用自己的血肉
餵養烏克蘭飢餓的兒童

以他們笨拙的大翅膀
舉身而飛
在他們被汙染的手上撒尿

以清除來自基輔死去的孩子
血液中的惡咒。

真正的詩人

真正的詩人
他一定要支持戰爭嗎？
他一定要嗎？
他一定要品嚐人們的死亡
流血
埋葬頭骨
他一定要嗎？
他一定要支持戰爭嗎？
他一定要嗎？
真正的詩人
他一定要嗎？
他一定要支持戰爭嗎？

真正的詩人
他一定要很高興看到人們尖叫嗎？
兒童挨餓
婦女哀嚎？

流離失所的人？
房屋空無一人？
廢墟下埋著老人？
他一定要嗎？
他一定要高興嗎？
他一定要嗎？
真正的詩人
他一定要嗎？
他一定要高興嗎？

他一定要支持戰爭嗎？
財產破壞
停電
糧食短缺
業務中斷
學校學習、
喪親之痛、損失

他一定要嗎？

他一定要支持戰爭嗎？

他一定要嗎？

真正的詩人

他一定要嗎？

他一定要支持戰爭嗎？

他一定要坐視

隨著建築物倒塌

大地在顫抖

硫磺導彈使地球凹陷

宇宙中嗡嗡作響的直升機

充滿無人機的日出

榴彈砲和裝甲運兵車篡改了日落

他一定要嗎？

他一定要坐視嗎？

他一定要嗎？

真正的詩人
他一定要
他一定要坐視嗎？

此時此刻

此時此刻我代表烏克蘭
她的男人和她的女人
她無辜的孩子們
我對你的愛
在霍韋爾拉山[*1]前展開
像無數瓣的蓮花
我為你流下的眼淚在眼眶裡燃燒
像第聶伯河的水一樣流動
我擁抱你，哦基輔！
我溫暖的吻，我充滿情感的擁抱
你是這個地球的孩子
不亞於丘陵和山谷
你屬於星星、月亮和天空
你的血液隨著多瑙河一起流淌
你心跳的韻律體現
在德涅斯特河[*2]的浪波峰上
你曾經出生在此

你會活下去，你會死去
帶走我的靈魂吧，哦，可愛的基輔！
我的想法和感受
我的想像和感情
將永遠住在霍韋爾拉山上。

[*1] 霍韋爾拉山（Mount Hoverla）：烏克蘭最高的山。
[*2] 德涅斯特河（The Dniester）：歐洲東部的一條河流，起源於烏克
　　蘭，注入黑海。當中部份河段為烏摩邊界。

死亡、悲傷和失落

聖母憐子圖

我跪在你面前哭泣
雖然死了
我能聽到你嘆息吐氣
的深沉呼嘯
痛苦的凝視
之刺眼存在
你搖晃的四肢
之無力掃蕩
你神聖的嘴唇
之咕噥嗚咽

我撫摸著你依偎在上面
的溫柔手臂
被蓋著
擦去守哀眼睛
的淚珠
以憐憫的溫柔觸摸

凹陷的臉頰
滿是皺紋的臉。

當我死去

當我死去時，我的親人
不要燒掉我的身體
也不要埋起來
讓它在地上腐爛

上面只要放一朵小花
但不是芬芳的玫瑰
因為我可能會聞到它並感到高興
並希望再活一次

當我不再呼吸時
我善良的兄弟姐妹
給我唱一首讚美詩中的歌
但是不要選擇十三這數字

因為它可能會在我耳邊吟唱
讓我冰冷的心變暖

回憶快樂的日子
讓我想再活一次

當我翹辮子時
我的身體變成赤裸的
給我讀聖經的一小段
但不要讀詩篇那一卷

因為你知道我是個罪人
對人類的貢獻甚微
並願意為慈善事業做點什麼
所以想再活一次

當我死去，美麗的世界
不要火葬我的屍體
別，用鋤頭，把我埋起來
讓它在地上變成廢棄。

凋零的玫瑰

我在籬笆上看到一朵玫瑰花
枯萎，樹葉黏在一起
就像一個人瘦弱的四肢
鬆弛並膚色蒼白

在多雨天氣裡衣衫襤褸
玫瑰冷冷地毫無生氣
我變得很傷心、想哭
想到它生命中的某一時刻

它接受了歡鬧的快樂和幸福
具有豐富的色彩、生命力和活力
身上帶著愛的象徵
情人為他們心愛的人挑選了它

現在它正在枯萎，生命從中流失
一個最終會死去的病人

淚水聚集在我的眼角
我想為死者哭泣和哀悼

突然一隻小蜜蜂飛進來
在花的上方盤旋了一會兒
它的低哼聲是輓歌，一個喪親之痛
的莊嚴表達，不可避免的喪失

它無法從枯葉上汲取花蜜
一團骯髒的深綠色，沒味道的溼氣
蜜蜂失望地飛走了，彷彿
從一具屍體離開，一具近乎腐爛的屍體

苦澀的淚水從我眼中滾落
我為失去而默默地哭泣，因為事實上
每一件美麗的事物，都必須在某時刻
腐朽而死，從地球上徹底消失

誰會知道我們曾在此？

知道我們曾經快樂而充滿活力地存在過嗎？

誰會記得我們色彩的美麗？

會如何解釋我們曾是生命和愛的源泉？

就躺在那裡

當你死去時，我親愛的朋友
不要試圖請願
不要問為什麼不能活久一點
或者，為什麼是你而不是別人
死去
就接受並離開人世

當他們把你藏進棺材時，親愛的朋友
不要抱怨
不要咕噥
或嘗試透過木箱窺視
想要活下去
就躺在那裡
因為你會在不一樣的空間
不一樣的時區
不一樣的存在

當他們圍著棺材尖叫時，親愛的朋友
不要和他們一起流淚
不要同情他們
只要旁觀著然後躺著不動
讓你的嘴保持張大
讓你的眼睛凝視
你的臉頰沉入嘴裡
你的牙齒露在你的嘴唇外
像隻疣豬
保持凍結狀態
保持枯萎
就躺在那裡

如果你聽到他們把你的身體放入土裡，親愛的朋友
不要抱怨
不要咕噥
或者嘗試破開棺材

對寒冷的居所
泥土築建的牆抗議
就躺在那裡
因為你會在不同的世界
不一樣的空間
不同的時區

當你開始腐爛分解時，親愛的朋友
不要捏住你的鼻子
也不要嘔吐
惡臭是新設計的一部分
蛆蟲是你的伴侶
蠕蟲是你的新親戚
沉默是新家的氛圍
孤獨是最終的宿命
就躺在那裡

煉獄

懸在這熾熱的報應空虛中，在
死亡和最後的歸宿間——在這種生存狀態下
我像貓一樣偷偷摸摸地移動，永遠站在他的腳趾
球；以貓的印象，冷漠超然，
我的臉耷拉著；我一點光都看不到。我喊叫，
「我要苦難和火！」

我來自的骯髒小村莊，聲音升起
為我的靈魂在這裡承受的痛苦和折磨而哭泣
意識到我的精神並沒有完全獨立於汙點
錯誤行為的世俗影響及其後果；兩者都不
邪惡到深淵的命運；但不斷
加強
靈魂本身在這裡是神聖的

沒有淨化——既沒有洗禮的聖禮，也沒有
懺悔——我的小罪孽沉重地壓在我的靈魂上
我為痛苦、火焰而哭泣，為神聖居所的獎賞而受苦

一個歡樂的花園。我要求解除我的
世上的行李；為了變完整之快樂的痛苦，去感受
祂的幸福奧祕

我發現自己處於那種思想和感覺的狀態
當現實讓位給遐想並與
煉獄第一階段的陰暗預知
我在溼冷的手上背負著輕微的罪惡，要清除
它們，這只是暫時的痛苦，然後不久我就要朝
奧林匹斯山[*1]走

它來了，像一聲雷鳴，或者像一個魔法咒語
一會兒光明，一會兒黑暗——一場大火！
明亮地燃燒，在我體內蔓延。我尖叫，「燒灼我！」
我聽到那些聚集在小村莊的人
來吧，歌唱，為我舉起他們的祭品——
以淨化。

[*1] 奧林匹斯山（Mount Olympus）：在希臘神話中為眾神居住的山。

凡人的靈魂

無情的長手將你帶走時
你將捨棄你的房子、汽車，你擁有的一切
一天天積累，辛辛苦苦付出的一切
一旦你走後，將被親戚擁有

你不會帶走任何東西，珠寶、一分錢都沒有
最好學會在沒有你擁有的美好事物的情況下生活
因為處於自私模式的土壤不會為你提供任何東西
但會讓你躺在那裡，空虛的，就像你出生時一樣赤身裸體

或者，更好的是，你可以嘗試死在加納
因為如果您在那兒是位知名的農民
你可以被埋在香蕉形狀的棺材裡
司機埋在公共汽車、木匠埋在木槌或錘子形狀內

至少這樣會讓你覺得有點值得
你不會後悔曾經這麼努力

而一下子失去了一切；如果你是一個吟遊詩人
你巨大的詩句檔案會在那裡，圍繞著你

但即使是那些西非人也沒有任何運氣
因為在土壤中時，你無法識別顏色
聖潔的白色、灰燼的灰色或葬禮的黑色
凡人的靈魂只知道花上的紅色。

蚊子

小東西，我的睡眠落於騷亂，沒有平靜
上床後，我討厭你在我頭上製造的噪音
但你不在乎，你繼續哀鳴和唱歌
好像你已經知道你很快就會死地呻吟

真如朝陽初升，我會確保你的死亡
我知道你的觸角已經嗅到我的汗味
你透過我身體的氣味、熱量和呼吸來定位我
你已經在我額頭上謀劃善巧地降落

但是，小東西，請注意，智慧屬於人類
不是你這種細腿小翅嗜血蟲
不要信任你匱乏的知識，哦，小東西：
使用視覺、嗅覺或熱提示的三重威脅

與人類的智慧相比，這算不了什麼
去找植物花蜜或蜂蜜對你來說是明智的

在花蜜或蜂蜜中，你可以獲得生存所需的糖分
並避免與人類進行不必要的決鬥

半睡半醒；嗡！有東西觸碰我的皮膚
我猜你的喙已經開始刺穿我的額頭
慢慢地，我感覺有個注射在我的肉體上，唾液滲入
哇！疼痛！我嚇了一跳──你快速地從我床飛走！

突然，我能聽到你帶著強烈的怨恨飛回來
我的手在半空中凍停，我聽到你慢慢地刺我的額頭
啪！粉碎！沉默接踵而來……小東西，你現在是汙泥
你永遠不會再試圖從我的頭上吸血

你永遠不會再嘗試從我頭吸血

我迅速從床上滑下來，打開房間的燈
手掌是紅色的──你已死──你再也不會叮人了

呸！討厭的蟲腸子！──我洗手並關燈
我現在可以期待今晚睡個無嗡嗡聲的覺了。

暮

——致祖母

弓著背
滿臉皺紋
咧嘴一笑
半瞎的眼睛
沒牙齒的嘴

你慢吞吞地走，奶奶
在你的手杖的支持下
進入黃昏
貓頭鷹過來為你唱歌
貓在你周圍咕嚕咕嚕跳舞

夜幕即降臨，奶奶
就像一個灰色的裹屍布
它將覆蓋地球
很快會暗了
我們不會在夜海中見到你

灌木叢會變成幽靈的形狀
河流聽起來怪異
月亮被烏雲遮住
你將迷失在黑暗的海洋中
我們不會再找到你了，奶奶。

墓地

頭莊嚴垂下
就像祈禱一樣
雙手張開
就像在一個誇張的擁抱中
四肢上
染血
釘子刺穿的洞
凌亂的髒頭髮
現在像劍麻一樣垂下

讓本丟彼拉多
在老鷹
俯衝到屍體上之前
讓十字架上的三個人下來
鬣狗咬牙切齒
成群結隊的蒼蠅
飄蕩的惡臭。

整個人生

整個人生
是麻煩
只有死亡
帶來安息

短暫的
像玫瑰一樣簡短
今天新鮮，開花
明天它枯萎

今天一個堅強的靈魂
明天一個悲傷的靈魂
搖搖欲墜
瓦解

生活的旋律使耳朵著迷
你喜歡跳舞

明天
旋律漸行漸遠

離開你
在地板上，側身
感覺
內部乾燥空曠

沒有什麼
讓人歡喜
整個人生旅程
是個麻煩。

當布幕落下

當布幕落下，身為悲劇英雄的我退場
不要驚恐地閉上眼睛並捂著臉頰
彷彿我不再存在，彷彿我突然變成了一個食人怪魔
沒有必要如此沮喪和如此狂怒

每天早上醒來，從臥室的窗戶偷看
在那裡，輪回再生！——我將成為你動物圍欄中的一隻山
羊
咩……！每天早上我都會咩咩叫、微笑並表達我的感受
我們的愛不會丟失，而在山羊和寡婦之間繼續

當火熄滅，只剩下餘燼和灰燼
不要突然畏縮、變冷、顫抖和抱怨
我會以蜥蜴之身回來，住在我們家的牆上
我們祕密交談，我們的愛情語言是悄悄話

我會每早起來曬曬太陽

在陽光下用我的尾巴和軀幹向你發出信號
這些行為會讓你記起過去的美好時光
我們曾多麼相愛、擁抱、親吻，以及我們所做的一切

當我的眼皮閉上、四肢凍定、並身體變僵硬
不要驚慌，而是用熱情和愛輕輕地把我釘進去
因為我會重生──我們的母牛會把我以一隻小牛生下我
你就完全沒有必要哀悼和悲傷

在圍場裡，我會蹲在我的臀部反芻
當你從欄圈潮溼的地板上鏟出糞便和泥土
我會在那裡快樂地微笑著並不時盯著你看
流口水是愛、善良、慾望和慾望的象徵

當暮光追上我而我戴著一條紅緞帶
不要被朋友的慰問淹沒
告訴他們，一切不是因死亡而結束

然後，有一天，我們母雞的蛋會裂開——在那兒，一隻雞
誕生了！

我將成為一個雛鳥住在養雞場作為你家庭的一員
當你向我扔糧丸時我會嘰嘰喳喳
告訴你，雖然曾隨風而去，但我又回來了
並我永遠都會，而死亡只是一個可悲的謬論

不要哭泣

如果我死了，不要哭泣
因為我會變成一朵玫瑰花
在你的花園裡生長
並散發著芬芳
你會在聖誕節期間摘下我
在生日時展示我
在婚禮儀式聞我
我會成為你的一部分
所以，如果我死了，不要哭泣

如果我死了，不要悲傷
因為我會變成一片南瓜葉
在你的菜園裡生長
晚上摘我當作晚餐
晚上在廚房裡烹調我
我會和你一起在餐桌上
所以，如果我死了，不要悲傷

如果我死了，不要呻吟
因為我會變成雨
從天而降
在排水溝旁收集我
用我洗廚房用具
我會在你的廚房
所以，如果我死了，不要呻吟

如果我死了，不要尖叫
因為我會變成一棵樹
在我們家園的一角生長
偶爾砍我當柴火
在你的廚房裡放一堆的我
用我生火煮烏嘎利[*1]
我將成為家庭的一份子
所以，如果我死了，不要尖叫。

[*1] 烏嘎利（ugali）：為東非的澱粉主食，玉米粉製成。

狹窄的道路

如果你渴望有一個家
在遠方的天堂
沿著狹窄的道路，隨著它的曲折
繼續走，儘管這是件厭煩的苦差事

但請記住這裡有誘惑
坐立不安可能會導致慘敗
就像羅得的妻子成為一堆鹽
並從那無形的慷慨之手中釋放治療

你可能會回頭看看
在那塗抹大地的汙垢之
淤泥中蠕動
滑下漫長而溼滑的道路

如果你渴望有一個家
扼殺你生命中的沉悶天氣

沿著狹窄的鵝卵石小路前行
像天使一樣得過且過

你會把其他人帶到那裡，自我克制
用奇特的語言交談
在脆弱的十字架下喘息
對未知喋喋不休的詛咒

回望黑暗的小村莊
艱難道路開始的地方
看看你居住的泥濘世界
其夜晚將你裹在死亡的命運中

上帝與神性

當我的身體枯萎

當我的身體枯萎
而我不再呼吸，主啊
給我翅膀飛翔
至煉獄之謎
在大海的
純淨的水中，主啊
讓我洗滌以淨化我的靈魂
給我一個較輕的懲罰，主啊
不是靈魂的拆解
身體被劇烈鞭打，主啊
而是臉上輕輕一巴掌
臉頰上捏一下，主啊
在我去奧林匹斯的路上
一路溫柔地載著我，主啊
上天堂的岩石山丘
下地獄的黑暗山谷
讓我到達您的居所，主啊

詭異的寂靜若隱若現
我可以在您的房間裡休息。

在我去奧林匹斯的路上

我的靈魂沉重地壓在
我的存在之良知
我踏上瓷磚門廊
帶著不敬虔的心
讓我在聖水缽[*1]的聖潔中
蘸我的手指
在我邪惡的外表上手劃十字
我在去奧林匹斯的路上
給我洗禮，懺悔
的聖餐
抵達煉獄後
用力鞭打我
給我澀苦的純潔之杯
蕩滌我的毀滅
輕輕地抱著我
沿著鵝卵石路
抵達您的聖地後
讓我在永恆的和平中安息。

[*1] 聖水缽：通常為天主教（教堂門口的）小聖水盆。

尋找祂

我鄭重地踏出我的路
尋找祂
以觸摸並感受祂神聖的質感
通常情況下，
我想念祂，發現我到達時
祂正要出發
但更重要的是，一如既往，
在很多方面，
我經常聽到祂的呼吸
在安靜的風的走廊裡
祂無形的存在
體現在黑暗的暴風雨之夜
之嚎叫、嗚嗚聲、
尖刺聲和尖叫聲中

在令人毛骨悚然的雷霆
爆裂聲中，在黑暗中

伸出祂的紅舌頭

鼓掌，抱怨

並喃喃自語

有時會引發

一棵著火的樹的濃煙，

一間房子或一個東西

表明祂的憤怒、暴怒，

因此，村里的老人，

殺山羊以安撫

社區所犯

罪惡或邪惡的行為

或者一些參與巫術

之化學的人

你可以找到祂

在祂的創造物中，在天空的海洋中

自由自在地游泳、漂浮

祂睜著一隻眼睛
不眨眼睛
堅持不懈地
在夜裡守望你
或者，早上
在地平線上展開祂的許多手指
為遠方那邊的山用
橙色油彩上色
祂的另一隻眼睛
閃閃發光，瞇著眼睛
在你打開臥室的窗戶時
或當你在田野裡拴山羊時對你微笑。

祂的缺席也是
祂隱形的存在
在花蕾上
當花瓣像是愛人的懷抱中打開時

感受創造的力量
成為祂所是的
美麗現象，或祂創造之物
立志成為的現象。

高草簇絨

我一直想知道
造物主所在
空氣和土壤的生命
高高豎起那些柱子
將蒼穹固定在原地；在疼痛中
讓自己哭泣出來以讓我們有雨。

我抬頭仰望天空
厚厚的雲層掛在那
藍天只有眩光
提供一點線索。

我走到河岸。
經過很多個世紀
創物的工作而疲憊，祂會在那裡
祂的身體清洗掉
大塊的灰塵；播放飛濺和潺潺聲

單調的，棕色的波浪
旋轉並攪動
但我沒有看到一個游到岸邊
的人之軀幹、腳趾。

在燦爛的憤怒中
我穿過黑夜的祕謎
為了碰到祂，煩惱
祂會反駁；
我的身影，月光洗滌下
的幽影，看見一個高大的黑影
向前彈跳
不是造物主的
不是天使的
而是一個絕望的凡人尋找真相之影。

我突然停下來聽著
風的輕柔歌曲，仔細地
一個一個採摘它的音符
感受節奏的轉調和不同的質感
突然──哎呀！祂的聲音
令人敬畏，但舒緩和關懷
慢慢地，詭異地從
深綠色的高草
簇絨中出現。

我今天想要什麼

今天我想
在太陽升起之前醒來
為新的一天讚美祂
虔誠、忠誠
達到淨化
清除邪惡的思想
惡意、嫉妒
嫉妒和諸如此類的東西
在這一天中
我要在我的臉上
帶著微笑，顯示
同理心和關懷
善待兄弟
扔一兩枚硬幣
至乞丐盤中
說一句
慰藉老人家的話

今天，我想
在太陽升起之前醒來。

有人掌控

在一個不眠之夜，我打開了
臥室小窗往外看以研究
夜晚之謎；一個黑暗的大池塘
填補世界的虛空。
我覺得它既鼓舞人心又令人敬畏
夜晚有一種方式讓你覺得世界上
任何地方都沒有生命存在，沒有上帝活著，
除了一片黑色的黑暗之外什麼都沒有
我們都可能已經死了。

當我呆呆地凝視著這片黑暗的池塘
一顆星星在天空某處探出頭來，然後逐漸地
月亮從厚厚的雲層中跳出來
像一個美麗的新娘騎著跨過天空
對站在窗邊的我微笑。
突然一顆流星驚人地從山坡上射下來
在想像的地平線上燃燒一條路徑
這是個有人掌握控制權之存在的標誌。

愛與美

你的全臉

一個人在這狹小的單人房
我坐著看著空蕩蕩的混凝土牆
我試著數數
投入建設它的
石頭的數量
試著想像讓牆壁發光的
粉刷工的名字
他的家庭背景
他的教育程度
他是如何扭曲佈滿皺紋的臉
以用他的畫筆作畫
他是如何咬著下唇
把畫筆在牆面往上推
他擺出的姿勢
以畫到房子的縫隙和角落
有時，我依著不知名的遠方音樂
不自覺地搖頭
無論是一隻鳥，還是

一支樂隊，或者一首
從過去回來的老曲調
或者，它可能純粹是，或也許是，虛構人物
在我腦袋裡打鼓
或者，有時，遠處傳來狗吠
我會不自覺地咬緊牙關
想像它在咬小孩
我六歲的女兒
害怕，我尖叫和悲傷
譴責和詛咒
有時，我閉上眼睛
讓我的思緒回到肯亞
給我們在學校的孩子們
到我們家
到布滿舊鞋的陽台
拖鞋、破衣服
去陽台的垃圾桶
在門廊嗡嗡作響的蜜蜂

聽到鄰居家的噪音
但一天中的大部分時間
我花時間看著格子窗外
期間我看到
田野裡的一叢矮樹
巨大的顫動的樹葉
露珠從灰色的樹枝上滴下來
看不見的風從他們身邊呼嘯而過
然後，慢慢地，逐漸地
你的綠色短裙，
帶黑色刺繡
和藍色條紋
出現，然後逐漸
你的眼睛，你的嘴唇
然後是你那張漂亮的臉。

（選自《Love from Afro-Catalonia》，2020年）

我愛你不像是……

我愛你不像是愛一塊巧克力
或像是芒果汁或香蕉水果或蘑菇
或像喜歡盤子裡的烤花生一樣
我愛你就像愛一個異國情調的夢
其中夢者穿著婚紗
而他的新娘美貌並容光煥發

我愛你不像是愛月光下的天空
或像是一棵高大的樹、或一片蔚藍的大海或夜空中的一顆
星
或像可以愛一隻蚱蜢、一隻白蟻或一隻蝴蝶
我愛你就像愛一束紅色的陽光
當早晨，像成熟的番茄，在地平線上綻放時
而昨夜的腳步早已遠去

我愛你不像是愛鳥巢裡之歌
或像是風的呼嘯聲或飛過的蜜蜂之嗡嗡聲

或像可以喜歡森林中一棵樹的口哨聲
我愛你就像愛住在海水中或住在墓地裡
的鬼魂之聲音
在夜間神秘的謎中聽到之起伏聲音

我愛你不像是愛新鮮咖啡的香氣
或像是生土或倒在坑裡的爛樹葉之氣味
或像可以愛上玫瑰或丁香樹的芬芳
我愛你就像愛愛人腋窩的味道
其色情質地和濃密毛髮的感覺
當她裸露時的潮溼和細流汗水

我愛你不像愛一件天才之作
或者看到一座在陽光下蔓延的壯麗城市
或像喜歡一雙新鞋、短褲或襯衫
我愛你就像愛一張破舊的照片
其中有一個在泥坑裡帶著純真、誠實
和虔誠的光環玩耍的孩子

今天早上

今天早上我
帶著失落感醒來
我發現寂靜占據了我房間的四個角落
還有一個謎
像是一位繆斯
在牆壁和空地之間
的光明和黑暗中玩耍

我從狹窄的床上滑下來
趕緊翻我的皮箱找你的照片
我一張都找不到
緊張的手指
向下滑動手機屏幕
我看不見一張——我的臉頰泛白

看著牆上的鏡子
我的嘴角形成了一個氣泡曲線

我的額頭像晴天一樣明亮
對家中的愛人
有慾的證據

現在坐在餐桌旁
我在一張紙上畫出你的身體
我愛的女人的想像
我內心的一種表達
我知道你對我的人

我用鉛筆畫上你的厚唇，讓你牙齒變白
牙齒，在你的胸前圈出雙丘
點綴你深沉感性的肚臍
我反覆在你的眼瞳上劃過
使它們膨脹，添加更多鉛筆
塗在臉頰上，讓它們耀眼迷人

遮住頭髮，使其有光澤
用兩條皺紋劈開你的額頭
（你不可能永遠年輕）
給你的鼻子一個暗影
你的下巴用淺色
然後用天鵝頸來穩定你的頭部

我坐下來檢查完成的作品
我的身體抽搐
我將嘴唇向下移動
親吻它
突然我聽到遠處傳來一聲響亮的嘆息
無聲的渴望
來自情人的淫蕩行為
用一句「我想你，哦，我的親愛」

（選自《Love from Afro Catalonia》，2020年，Kistrech Theatre
International）

看著她

我看著她
將她的身體攤開在一張白色的床單上
她是一望無際的藍色大海
布滿點點的星星
華麗的
可口的
她的嘴唇和我的
在新月的某個地方
找個位置
鎖定對方
光色變暗
我們的心打結糾纏
在我們夢幻般的世界
中間。

我很快就要回家了

我一個人在奧洛特[*1]，我不想再一個人了
我想盡快回家，我親愛的
我想見你、想吻你、想愛你
觸及你的嘴唇、你的舌頭和你的牙齒

我想盡快見到你，我最親愛的
我想念你，想再次與你聯繫
與你相遇，伸手觸及你的呼吸
你的氣味、你的香氣、你的汗水和你的異味

我受過寂寞、思念、願望和渴望
我想為了你回家到你身邊，親愛的
坐在陽台看夜空
和你一起數天空碗裡的星星

我想盡快回家，我親愛的
再一次，就像我們過去一直做的那樣

灰暗的夜晚一起去田野裡走
捉白蟻、蝴蝶和蚱蜢

我不想再留在奧洛特了，我的親愛
想回家看夜雨
再次享受屋頂上的敲擊音樂
還有我們屋外形成的泥濘水坑

我真的很想回家，我最親愛的
看到你的頭髮、你的臉、你的脖子、你的胸部
看看你的裙子、你的襯衫和你的腰帶
看看你的內衣、胸罩和睡衣

我想念你也愛也想和你在一起
我想聆聽你的聲音，因為它總是出現在我身邊
我想聆聽你的咯咯笑聲和笑聲
聆聽你如何打嗝、打噴嚏、發噴噴聲、吸氣和打鼾

我想回家和你一起去田野裡走
聆聽鳥巢中鳥兒的歌聲
然後我們走在樹林裡聽你唱歌給我聽
牽手、擁抱、擁抱和親吻

我們一起在黑夜裡捉螢火蟲
並將其視為浪漫和愛的行為
像我們一直做的那樣把它們放在一個小籃子裡
看著它們像你閃爍的眼睛一樣閃爍著光芒

每一天我都想像著從西班牙的奧洛特出發
離開這個房間，這沉悶的天氣
結冰的池塘、寒冷的道路和多雪的山
回家享受陽光和溫暖的細雨

*1 奧洛特（Olot）：為西班牙加泰隆尼亞赫羅納省的一個市鎮。

我著迷

我因
臀部周圍
曲線著迷
肚臍
的
深度
你
腹部
的渾圓
溫柔的下降
沿著
灌木叢的
樹林的田野
來到
喜悅的
湧泉
興奮的
溪流

我40歲的妻子

花朵
已經脫落
玫瑰
這有點快
恐慌的
苛求的
40在你下面點了一把火
精神病起痟的動作
緊張的
非理性行為
斷線效應
生活的泥潭
謙卑地涉過。

你把它像戴在脖子上的鍊子戴著

你內心的戰爭才剛剛開始
哦可愛的
它的輸出很容易追蹤到
在腹部周圍的脂肪中
你胸部的溫柔
我可以從你臉上的壓抑和焦慮
衡量它的嚴重性
情緒低落
過敏反應
還有多段的哭泣。
你的痛苦在我的血管中沸騰
我變得疲倦
我和你一樣晚上出汗
晚上沿著牆壁摸索
去廁所
經常和你一起小便
這對你來說是一個新常態，

這對我來說是一個新常態
我好像很懂你
我經常站在你的立場
我知道其中的痛苦
萎縮性陰道炎
你把它就像戴在脖子上的鍊子戴著
這是一條所有女人都會走的路
那個內在的渴望
被無欲之風帶走
性交困難
薄陰唇
痛苦的路徑
焦慮
這是一條我們倆都走的黑暗道路。

紅色情緒的汙點

看一眼

你的內褲

看到

紅色情緒的汙點

畫到你的存在

之畫布上

帶著七風的汙漬

它們的翅膀載著

在你身內

狂奔而出的惡魔。

他們把我們像樹上的枯葉一樣吹走

紅色的耍性子

憤怒

喧囂

動盪。

在你自己的中心

在你自己的中心
你是一個魯蛇
緊緊抓住那些卷鬚
彷彿世界
從它們葉子的祕密部分滑落
鳥兒歌唱著
你尚未掌握的英雄氣概
你是折斷翅膀的天使
正於下半旗的高度飛翔
你走了，只是現在
我想知道你明天會變成什麼樣：
當日蝕將太陽擋住時
築巢的鷦鷯？
或，一隻掌握了四季的織鳥
將它的夢一些碎片餵給她的雛鳥？
讓我帶你去雲端
生命如此依賴於它的神秘之美

用你漏水的夢之碎片
裝飾天空、空氣和風
至少現在你已經成為
大祭司，製造雨滴
的雌雄同體
是下一代的祝福
但把你神聖的雙身軀
跨坐在兩個熟悉但分開的世界上。

致達米亞娜

如果性讓我快樂，請給我
你不要像麝和米飯一樣吝嗇
讓我慢慢墜入並看到美色
當我開始上升時讓你嘆息和微笑
如果性讓我興奮，允許我進來
穿過你的珍珠、銀和金之門
達到前所未有的快樂
並學會講述一個從未被講述過的故事
如果我真的愛性，請也愛它
支持我繼續航行去尋找
為兩人點燃的火焰寶藏之歸宿
為我們的靈魂加熱並點燃它們
因此，讓我們游泳並到達海底
當大海紅色黏糊糊旋轉時唱著歌

如果我堅持要它，慷慨點，親愛的
不要在你漂亮的臉上戴著皺紋

或透過顯示一些恐懼來表示不喜歡
試試抹去你眼中的惡意
因此，親愛的，請允許我去海濱
指觸海草，撓海甘藍癢
海獅伸出它的灼熱繩帶
看著它變成可出海的，腫脹的雄性
親愛的，請讓我們暢通無阻
沿著海道砍掉海藻
駛向燃燒海底的帆船
我的世界這邊又那邊地搖擺不定
當我完好無損地躺在這遙遠的海底
蜷縮在海邊——請抱住我的頭！

離開家

今天早上我離開家時
我們站在門口
就像兩個陌生人在一個可怕的時刻中

互相凝視
你的指甲塗了清漆
明亮系的紅色

你穿的粉紅色女牛仔裝
讓你的臉消瘦變窄
你大大的、垂瞼的雙眼

整齊的白齒，亂糟糟的頭髮
像劍麻一樣立在你的頭上——
給了你不剃鬚的青春魅力

我記得貓出來

在我們的雙腿之間挖幾個洞
你靠得更近了，你的手

我周圍有一大片羊毛和毛皮
我們接吻了；你口齒不清
淚如灼燒的雨落下

我感到胸口溼漉漉的溫暖
你用尖銳的小女孩語氣說
在哥倫比亞時要小心。

突如其來的愛情

我帶著失落感醒來
找到一片溫柔的寂靜
持著我臥室的四個角落

我抬頭看到她的臉
從牆上的照片往下看
我們的目光糾纏在一起
星星進入我的視野

我突然感到突如其來的愛
從溫暖的床單中升起
輕輕地灑進我的心裡
穿過我的眼睛向上推進
填滿我的整個大腦

然後慢慢自我組裝
以多個分流的溫柔微笑和色情嘆息

柔和地溢出
並歸結是它
來自的床單。

讓我知道

如果我曾冒犯你
和我討論，親愛的
不要把這藏在心裡太久
讓我知道我犯的
錯誤，親愛的
這讓你臉色蒼白、啞口無言
如果我曾對你大喊大叫
而你心慌意亂，親愛的
那是因為我在乎，或我是這麼認為的
讓我們以開放的心態來談
那些缺陷、陷阱
並修補破損的柵欄
以結束沉默
再次聽到你的聲音，親愛的
就像之前它都一直來找我的樣子。

你的到來

當我聽到大門吱吱作響
砰砰聲，通往廣場的小徑旁
青草沙沙作響，突然的
寧靜，然後，慢慢地，鑰匙轉動門孔
我只知道是你的到來

但在大多數情況下
這只是一種錯覺

路過的風可能想要沙沙作響
草或蜥蜴不小心掉到
水泥門廊上，翻身狂奔
穿過小徑，聽起來像有人急著回去
嘿！我喊出口，卻只有房間裡空蕩蕩
的回聲回應我

我已經歷過數次的到來
你的到來
還有那些回聲，像難以捉摸的夢
一樣降臨在我身上
並使我的感情虛假地興高采烈。

新生的

有個東西，是新生的
已經開始
爬它的坡度

在其攀登時
它觸動心靈的閣樓
灑下它的香氣

當我傾斜我的思維框架
它在牆上反彈
分散我的思緒

眼花繚亂！──我喜歡它
它讓心靈充滿魅力
和魅力

它不斷地凝固
婉約甜美
壓倒性的魅力。

蜂蜜涌上的暮光：
漢英雙語詩集

走出隔離

宵禁時間！

宵禁時間到了
哦，快點——快點！
警察在街角
各自定位
準備要戰鬥
婦女們匆忙疊好她們的商品
並趕往倉庫
當人們從市場跑回家時
孩子們在媽媽背後尖叫
宵禁時間到了！

馬塔圖[*1]飆過去
鳴叫與嗶嗶聲
音樂喇叭大響
I say a hip! A hap! A hip to the hippie!
You don't stop to rap to the bang bang boogie!
I rap to the beat nobody can rap!

裡面的人用手掌托著頭
痛苦地閉上眼睛
並詛咒司機。
一個行人漫不經心地橫穿馬路
差點被超速駕駛者撞到
街頭男孩利用喧囂：
鬥爭
刮痕
致殘
搶奪
一個包包、一支手錶、一支手機
消失在高樓後面
進入黑暗狹窄的小巷
宵禁時間！

博達博達[*2]
一次接載兩名乘客

一次三個
一次四個
在路上俯衝
像一隻老鷹
嗶嗶聲
呼喊著
咆哮中蜿蜒穿過
在人行道上行駛
讓路！移開！讓路！移開！
瘋子會喊著
導致行人驚惶奔跑地逃命
宵禁時間！

商店門吱吱作響
和撞擊聲
格柵百葉窗向下滾動
並砰的一聲

擊中水平混凝土底座
業主衝出去
袋子在他們的肩膀上擺動
迅速進入他們的汽車並飆走
遠山揚起塵埃
天空的藍色圓頂變成棕色
宵禁時間！

看到一個老人
快快地，跋涉回家
用拐杖支撐自己
他的嘴巴快速地張開和閉上
自言自語
庫羅納[*3]！庫羅納！哦庫羅納！
他詛咒和譴責
他搖頭
憤怒和痛苦使他的額頭皺起

宵禁時間！

呦威伊！呦威伊！呦威伊！
警笛聲切斷了空氣
哭泣，就像新冠葬禮上的那些老婦人
人們爭先恐後
道路被封鎖
歪曲、賄賂、罰款、監禁
一個巨大的咆哮
喇叭鳴喇叭！
喇叭號角聲！
詛咒！譴責！
新冠苦難是極度的困擾
誒！宵禁時間！

（發表於《Between the Walls and Empty Spaces》，Demer
Press，荷蘭，2022年）

*1 馬塔圖：改為計程車的小巴士。
*2 博達博達：東非的摩托車計程車。
*3 庫羅納：新冠病毒（corona）的口誤。

什麼顏色？

我可以用什麼顏色
畫你的名字，哦新冠？
像結冰之雪
的白色？
還是像血一樣的紅色？
如果我用像裹屍布
的黑色
畫你的名字呢？
還是像棺材一樣的棕色？
讓我用像
像柴堆
的灰色
或像悲傷大海
的藍色畫這名字。

最可能
我可以用像墳墓

的土褐色
帶有灰色條紋
在你嬌嫩的背部和手臂上
像沉悶的雲畫你的名字。

垃圾堆

每天我開車經過這裡
我打開窗戶
允許惡臭
輕鬆飄入
測試是否
我的嗅覺仍然完好無損
而且我沒有變成陽性。
如果我沒有聞到
從垃圾堆中飄出的氣味
我就知道我已經
染上了微小的微生物
並除了透過
祈禱和免疫力的窗戶
我無路可逃。
所以我一直把鼻子
探出窗戶
在吸入惡臭
好讓自己能繼續活下去。

好事即臨的預兆

世界不再顫抖

起伏

輾過自己

像一個受驚的孩子，大喊大叫

尖叫地遠離陌生人

有明顯的平靜

在天體宇宙

紅色的血跡

被神雨沖刷下來

恐怖的氣息

漂浮在宇宙中

被掃入

風的寧靜走廊

拼命哀嚎

呼嘯、譴責

在場的那者，

也是神秘的不存在

天體宇宙中的哨兵

把星星丟到我們面前，就像來自天堂的五彩紙屑

我們伸展我們溼冷的手掌

請願和暫時擱置

照顧我，哦，恩祠琛[1]

照顧我，哦，恩祠琛

以及星團落在我們的手上

的聲音是舒緩的

還有悶燒的雨

的嗡嗡聲

溫柔的雷雨

燦爛的閃電，蟋蟀的叫聲

通常會與河流潺潺的水聲交融

而交談的林木

似乎在對鳥兒的呢喃低語

和平與和諧

充實和豐富的生活

——好事即臨的預兆。

*1 恩祠琛（Engoro）：為肯亞基西人原始信仰中的主神。

我來到內羅畢

我今天早上來到內羅畢

來看新冠

我聽說它穿著高跟鞋

走在街上

像個竊賊

戴著兜帽

像個十幾歲的男孩

把口罩戴歪

它像患狂犬病的無牙狗一樣狂吠

它尖端有刺的尾巴

在兩腿之間搖擺

它的眼皮抿在一起

沮喪

害羞、膽小

就像一個被迫面對割禮者的刀

的 12 歲鄉村男孩

他厭惡的儀式

卻要像帶著過去的傷去拳擊場
的一個著名拳擊手經歷
然而他的支持者大喊大叫
配著震耳欲聾的掌聲

今天早上我來到這個城市
因好奇感到不安
來看新冠
我聽說它在街上奔跑
以驚人的速度
當它聽到輕微的聲音時
它停下來，在人行道上腳步錯亂
多次摔倒自己，
像松鼠一樣吱吱叫
它看人的眼神就好像希望它能生活在地球上一樣
大多數時候
它飛向稀薄的空氣
在人行道上留下它的液狀影子。

彎腰撿起它的舊布

恐怖和恐懼

警報聲

正在快速變弱

減少、已消失或即將消失

微生物的致命爪子

不再可怕

神聖使者的

溫柔腳步

聽得到那邊的

守護靈

盛開的花朵在我們的腦海中生長

我們用眼睛捕捉

陽光的柔和影像

瞥見月光下的夜晚

文靜地燃燒的蠟燭

聆聽鳥兒輕柔的嘰嘰喳喳

早晨了

夜晚像粉筆一樣瓦解
黎明已逝
或者即將走了
人們開始聚集在街上
擁抱和親吻
沒有口罩的面孔表現出笑聲和咯咯笑聲
生活已經回來，或即將豐盛的
回來
衝進來，彎腰撿起它的舊布。

走出隔離

不要疲倦，也不要吸入
絕望的氣息
或黑暗的悲觀主義
恐懼的季節
現在在我們身後
春天在那邊
新希望之萌芽
開始在我們的自我
核心內成長
新的火焰冒出
陽光
在山上是明亮的
鳥兒又能唱歌了
田野上長滿了新鮮的草
地球恢復生機
擁抱
接吻

聚會
一個新的開始
一個春天的季節

（首次發表於《Spring's Blue Ribbon：International Poems》，
由 Gino Leineweber 編輯，VerlagExpeditionen，2021）

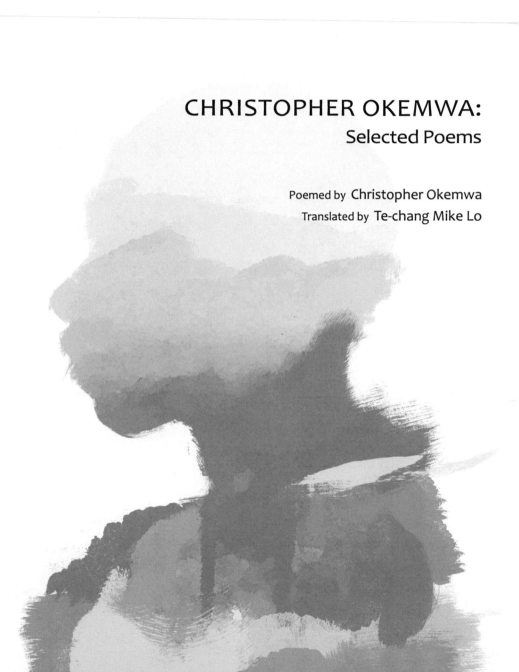

CHRISTOPHER OKEMWA:
Selected Poems

Poemed by Christopher Okemwa
Translated by Te-chang Mike Lo

CONTENTS

Chapter 7　Coming out of Isolation／走出隔離

Chapter

Nature and Beauty

1

The Wind

I hear you singing, swishing
and wheezing in all direction
shaking and blowing off thatch
roofs from huts in dereliction

Squeezing through a dense bush
forest, newly-cut hedgerow
raging all the way, settling in
a dark glade with a blazing row

You lift confetti, festoon and old
sacks, scattering them in the sky
you then pick light clothes from
the line as you whine and cry

Hurling them on tarmac roads
paths, bushes and fields afar

flutters and whirrs about fuzzy flags,
spiralling up fluffs and fur

You enter our bedroom through an
open creaking window on the wall
disrupts mosquito nets and window
swags in your mischievous prowl

Rumples blankets and bed sheets,
stirring crockery on the bed-side table
leaving the room with a tremble,
a whine, and a soft danceable treble

Sometimes you waft along, silently,
swallowing your anger and pride
listening, one might think you have
dropped down, fainted and died

But suddenly leaves outside go
nodding, fluttering and fidgeting
then one realizes that you are alive,
whistling a tune that is riveting

In gusts, you are always back
with gusto, among trees grumbling
gurgling through thick hedgerows;
a guiro, whining and rumbling

Gratuitous, leaving behind broken
boughs, scattered twigs and foliage
telling of your wreaking power,
a mighty fury, a flaunting proud rage

The Amazing Night

Sometimes I get so amazed when I watch the night
The way stars drop in on the dark bowl of the sky
And the moon clad in its burnished silver-streaked white
Peeps and hides behind sheep of clouds like a spy

I look at this one sheet of Black - a mass of darkness
I find it a mystery that suffuses me with fear and horror
From its dark hollow space, its endless sea of emptiness
Could easily spring out a demon, an imp or a giant ogre

Or something simply wicked, malevolent and evil
That could devour me, consume or take away my soul
So I always peep thru the window to be sure no such devil
Spills into the room in its formidable amorphous prowl

I find it hard to imagine how the night comes to be:
The ominous silence that keeps vigil in every mini space
The opaque black that blinds eyes so that they don't see
Its black furs and grey paints that make an intricate maze

The night is like a churning sea, an agitating ocean
I always see it spilling through the window on the wall
Submerging me in my bedroom in its furious motion
Suffocating and choking me up, leaving dead my soul

I get scared to imagine that someone, out of ill intention
Might one night get access to the giant clock of the universe
Then hold the gadget from moving, against Deity's creation
Shall we live in darkness forever?-what hell shall be for us!

Twilight on the Mead

There is silence in the mead, deep and sweet
Perfumed by sprawling blooms of chrysanthemums
The soft twilight lay fermenting on the green lush

Peace and fulfillment drape over clumps of shrubs
And the wooden paling and ripening guava trees
Veil in the aura and beauty of an orange sunset

The growing maize plants and finger millet
Kiss the thick jacket, embrace the warm slacks
Sorghum salute amicably as I scuffle across

Dots of vultures decorate the washed-blue welkin
Floating lazily through the air; the sky is clear
The moon is now rising, pale, but almost round.

Idyllic

Walk past the bushy-paved corner

Come to an embarrassing sight:

A rustic codger, his chin as bushy as his milieu

Squatting in shallow clumps of shrub

Wild-eyed, stooling; his face

A ballad, manifesting vividly the sort

Of place our childhood was dissipated

Go further on and a stark nude

Little brat will squelch across the muddy road

The pendulum of history

Beating before the shrine of procreation

Telling what we were in days of yore

In the gloaming at the beer party meet dishevelled

Fogey mothers whose haunches will loosely

Be cased in menstruation-stained lesos

Listen to their jumble of conversations

Innuendoes, humour and laughter

Spend your night on a sisal mat, wake

Up in the morn with a lingering headache

Crows, bleats and lows charging your morning air

You will need a pair of thick boots

To wade through the midden-ridden path

As you leave the village.

The Gong

Of my childhood rings louder
Its echo hurtles in, faster
Catching up with me
Every night in my dreams

The bicycles, donkey-carts
The farmers' open vans
Raced up and down this pebbly road
Leaving behind trails of dust

I sat here, on this anthill
On a market day
Counting people, donkeys
I was a loner then
The mantis as my teddy bear.

The Earth

Oblate Spheroid

Or flat like a ruler

Or round like a ball

It doesn't matter

Whether ridges, slopes, or knolls

Deform its scalp

Or valleys, dales

Make a dent on its amorphous skin

It doesn't matter

Mine is a standard space

A 6ft long by 6ft deep rectangular world

In which to wrap my soul

In the most glittering colours

Red flowers and red ribbons

It really doesn't matter

Oblate Spheroid

Or flat like a ruler

Or round like a ball

Mine is a small space

A 6 by 6 rectangular world.

The Gloaming

Colours

of the evening

are now fermenting

Waiting

to melt

into a nightball

The dark

is yet to touch

the ground

It is women's eyes

The cosmos

Is filled with chirps, trills

The wind blows

Gently

The earth, slowly, go to sleep.

This Morning

I sit on the tall dew-clad grass

Sewing through random thoughts

How beautiful life could be

The morning sun is bewitching

An adorned wedding bride

She forms a provocative outline behind the trees

The rays are piercing

Like an arrow of a Maasai Moran

Splashing orange paints on the hills

And colouring the sky in white-washed blue

Staring simply at me below

How beautiful life could be

The wind is gentle on my skin

Tufts of grass bend over one another

Dew glues them, one on another

Making them lovers in an embrace

The bee hovers above the flowers

Flits away, then flits back

Suckling and slobbering upon the nectar

How beautiful life could be

Chapter

Politics and Politicians

On the Podium of Lies

His sugar-coated tongue

A serpent's fangs

Lethal to the society

A Biblical Zacchaeus

Greed for material wealth

His pose on the podium

Hands banging the lectern

An Iago, a crooked evil image

With power to control

To destroy, not only Othello, Roderigo,

Emilia, Desdemona

But himself and the society

Look at his skewed eyes

A leaf of dishonesty flutter in the pupils

Like Abimelech of Shechem

Ambition, like a restless acid

Burns in his animal heart

There is a mark of Cain

On his fiery forehead

A piece of bread on one hand

A double-edged sword on the other

To destroy souls, to shed blood

Be aware, good people

Become Jotham and run -- vote him out

Hear what he tells the crowd

He doesn't even listen to himself.

(Published in *Madnes: An Anthology of Worlds Poetry*, WPM-Nepal, 2022)

They Are Here With Us

Be careful, be alert and be aware

The dark angels are here with us

Always appearing during election period

Driving fuel-guzzling

Tinted, thick-tired

Ferraris, Aston Martins

Alfa Romeos, Bugattis

Rolls-Royce Phantoms

Roaring about like a pack of wolves

Thirst for the voter's blood

The sky -- dotted with helicopters!

They fly above us like gods

Mr. Moneyberg! Mr. Moneyberg!

The worshippers below get frenzy

He is flattered, he feels himself a hill

Drops and sprinkles note-money

Like manna from the heavens

Voters buy into his avalanche of lies

His opulence, his stolen wealth

They swim in a sea of his riches

Choking on his false pledges

Stumbling on his promises

I will construct the libraries!

I will build class rooms in schools!

I will install electricity to every home!

I will pay fees for damn poor children!

Be careful, be alert and be aware

He is a camouflaged snake

Slithering in green grass

Born by the bolted Lucifer

Bearing a tongue of silver

A lethal tail, poison at the tip

Sharp-pointed horns on his temples

Claws, a double blade machete

Be careful, be alert and be aware.

CHRISTOPHER OKEMWA:

Selected Poems

170

Chapter

War and Peace

3

War Is Like...

War is a rotten egg
that bursts broken
Splashing its ordour
before our facades and faces
We run, choking
pinching our nostrils tightly
leaving behind
traces of our broken tears
Our mortal footsteps
Sink beneath the earth
Stained with trails of blood
We inter our
Parents' souls and bones
and cover their grey wisdom
with rubble and soil
We carry the ash
of our children's dreams

blowing them off like wind

And on the pyre

we smoke up the soul of the generation

of our grand children

(Published in *UKRAINE: A World Anthology of Poems on War*, Ed.

Christopher Okemwa, 2023)

Must You Tell Your Mother?

——A Poem for the Warriors in Our Community

When the war has began

Must you tell your mother?

You coward

You dog of a boy!

You lazy-for-nothing lad!

A curse to the community

A shame to the young generation

Must you tell your mother?

Must you?

Must you tell your mother?

When the battle-horn is blown

And the entire village stirs

Women gather arrows and line up spears

Men paint their skins with ochre, clay and soot

Must you linger about?

Must you stand lazily undecided?

Must you?

Must you gaze emptily confused?

Must you turn your head back to your mama?

What kind are you?

Who carried you in her womb?

Whose tit did you suckle?

Who reared you in her lap?

Which knife slashed your foreskin?

You dog of a boy!

You coward lad!

Must you?

Must you tell your mother?

When the battle-drum is beaten

And the warriors line up for death and for life

And the enemy lurks behind Nyangweta forest

Should you look back to find your mother?

Should you?

Should you seek advice from your mother?

Oh coward of cowards

Oh curse of curses

Should you seek for your mother?

Should you?

Should you seek for your mother?

When the other lads are out

Drums reverberating from every corner of the village

Dancers shaking the ground on Manga ridge

Cows bellowing

Goats bleating

The fields awash with ululations

And the riverbanks broken by war chants

And the people talking in innuendoes

Must you not understand parables of our people?

Must you look dumb?

Must you lag behind?

Must you be in the hut warming your *egesena*?

Oh coward of cowards!

Oh curse of curses!

Should you lag behind?

Should you tell your mother?

NOTE: Egesena, a traditional piece of cloth in the Abagusii community in Kenya tied around the waist to cover the front part of the person's private parts.

(Published in *Culture & Identity, Vol 1 WORLD,* Compiled by Robin Barratt, Published by THE POET, ISBN: 9798414877431, 2022)

Ukraine

Bullets and bombs
Rumble in Ukraine like thunderstorms
Our ancestors turn in their graves
Wailing, their tears
Flood in to fill the Dnieper

The morning sunlight
Illuminate shadows of lethal ghosts
The horizon is red
Blood of heroes colour the skylines
Above the Hoverla and Brebenskul
The music of birds in Uholka-ShyrokyiLuh
Fades slowly in the primeval beech forest

The stars at night
Unveil the fire of bullets
The song of the wind moan for Ukraine

On its own winged lips, it carries

Secrets of the enemy yonder

Flowers

Spring out like bullets

Meteors shoot down the sky like bombs

Ashes, smoke, rocks and dust

Combine to bury the dead.

(Published in *UKRAINE: A World Anthology of Poems on War*, ed. Christopher Okemwa, 2023)

Old Buzzards

With broad wings

Expansive rounded tails

Floating on updrafts of air

Cycling over Kyev

High up in the sky

Is this presence ironic?

Does it symbolize a rebirth?

So, then, are we to

Release ourselves to the winds

And fly with the buzzards?

With their nostrils wide open

They smell cow manure

Grasshoppers, dead snakes

With their curved beak wide open

They sight small bugs

Dead skunks and chicks

They take a swoop

Noise of howitzers, anti-tank grenades

Smoke of bombs, dust from rockets

Wails and screams are heard below

Having had enough carcasses

Gorged

They can't fly

Part of them lose life

Oh Moscow

Regurgitate

To feed Ukraine's hungry children

With their own blood and flesh

With their large clumsy wings

They lift themselves up

Urinating on their tainted hands

To clean off the evil spell

Gotten from blood of Kyev's dead children.

A True Poet

A true poet

Must he support war?

Must he?

Must he savour in the dying of people

The shedding of blood

The burying of skulls

Must he?

Must he support war?

Must he?

A true poet

Must he?

Must he support war?

A true poet

Must he be glad to see people screaming?

Children starving

Women wailing?

People displaced?

Homes deserted?

Old people buried under the rubble?

Must he?

Must he be glad?

Must he?

A true poet

Must he?

Must he be glad?

Must he support war?

The destruction of properties

The power outage

The food-shortage

The disruption of businesses

School learning,

The bereavement, the loss

Must he?

Must he support war?

Must he?

A true poet

Must he?

Must he support war?

Must he sit back and watch

As buildings come tumbling down

The earth trembling

Brimstone missiles denting the earth

The cosmos buzzing with helicopters

Sunrises filled with drones

Sunsets tampered with howitzers and APCs

Must he?

Must he sit back and watch?

Must he?

A true poet

Must he

Must he sit back and watch?

Here Now

Here now I stand for Ukraine

Her men and her women

Her innocent children

My love for you

Unfolds itself before Mt. Hoverla

Like a Lotus of countless petals

My tears for you burn in my eyes

And flow like waters of the Dnieper

My embrace for you, oh Kyev!

My warm kisses, my emotional hug

You are a child of this earth

No less than the hills and the valleys

You belong to the stars, the moon and the sky

Your blood flows with the Danube

The rhythm of your heart-beat is embodied

On the crest of the waves of the Dniester

And here then you were born

And you will live, and you will die

Take my soul with you, oh lovely Kyev!

My thoughts and feelings

My imaginations and affections

Will live on Mt. Hoverla forever.

Chapter

Death, Grief and Loss

4

The Pieta

I kneel before you, sobbing
Although dead
I can hear the profound whizz
Of your sighing breath
The piercing presence
Of a painful gaze
The feeble sweep
Of your wobbling limbs
The mumbling whimper
Of your sacred lips

I touch the tender arms
On which you are nestled
Tucked in
Wipe drops of tears
Off the eyes that mourn
Touch with piteous softness

The wrinkled face
The sunken cheeks.

When I Die

When I die, my fair kin
Don't burn my body
Don't bury it either
Leave it to rot on the ground

Only put a little flower on it
But not the fragrant rose
For I might smell it and be happy
And wish to live again

When I breathe no more
My kind siblings
Sing me a song from the hymnal
But don't choose number thirteen

For it might chant my ears
And warm my cold heart

Be reminiscent of joyful days

Making me wish to live again

When I kick the bucket

And stark becomes my body

Read me a little line from the bible

But don't read the psalms

For you know I am a sinner

And have done little to mankind

And would want to do something for charities

Therefore wishing to live again

When I die, my fair world

Don't cremate my body

Don't, with hoes, inter me either

Leave it to waste on the ground.

A Withering Rose

I saw a rose flower at the hedgerow
Withering, leaves stuck together
Like skinny limbs of a human being
Flaccid and of pallid complexion

Bedraggled in the rainy weather
The rose had become coldly lifeless
I became so sad and felt like crying
Thinking that at one time in its life

It was open to hilarious joy and happiness
With richness of colour, life and vitality
Carried on its body the symbol of LOVE
And swains picked it for their beloveds

Now it was wilting, life juicing out of it
A sick person who eventually would die

Tears gathered at the corner of my eye
I wanted to sob and grieve for the dead

Suddenly a small bee came flitting in
Hovered for a while above the flower
Its hum a dirge, a solemn expression
Of the bereavement, the inevitable loss

It couldn't get the nectar upon the fading leaves
A Sordid mass of dark green, tasteless wetness
The bee flew away in disappointment, as if
From a carcass, a near-decomposed corpse

Bitter tears rolled down from my eyes
I sobbed silently for the loss, for the fact that
Every beautiful thing, at one time, must
Decay and die, vanish completely from the earth

Who will then ever know we were here?

That we once joyfully and exuberantly existed?

Who will recall the beauty of our colours?

Explain how we were a source of life and love?

Just Lie There

When you die, my dear friend

Do not try to petition

Do not ask why you can't live longer

Or, why you and not someone else

Died

Just accept and pass on

When they stash you in the coffin, dear friend

Do not grumble

Do not mumble

Or try to peep through the wooden box

Desiring to live on

Just lie there

For you will be in a different space

A different timezone

A different existence

When they scream around the casket, dear friend

Do not shed tears with them

Do not sympathize with them

Just look on and lie still

Let your mouth stay gaping

Let your eyes stare

Your cheeks sink into your mouth

Your teeth stick out of your lips

Like a warthog

Remain frozen

Remain withered

Just lie there

If you hear them lowering your body to the soil, dear friend

Do not grumble

Do not mumble

Or try to break open the casket

To protest the cold abode

The soil-made walls

Just lie there

For you will be in a different world

A different space

A different timezone

When you start to rot and decompose, dear friend

Do not pinch your nose

Do not throw up either

Stench is part of the new design

Maggots your companion

Worms your new kith and kin

Silence the ambience of the new home

Loneliness the ultimate destiny

Just lie there

Purgatorius Ignis

Hanging in this burning emptiness of retribution, between

Death and the final dwelling--in this condition of existence

I move stealthily like a cat, perpetually on the balls of his

Feet; with the cat's impression, indifferent aloofness,

My face drooped; in my eyes no light at all. I cry,

"I want affliction and fire!"

The soiled hamlet from whence I have come, voices rise

To cry for the pain and torture that my soul bore here

Aware that my spirit is not fully independent of the stains of

Mundane effects of wrong-doing, its consequences; neither

Sufficiently evil to be fated for abyss; but keeps on strengthening

Itself in sanctity here

Having no purifications -- neither sacrament of baptism, nor

of penance -- my venial sins weigh heavy on my soul

I cry for pain, fire, to suffer for the rewards of the divine abode

A Garden of delights. I ask to be relieved of my

Earthly baggage; for the pain of joy to be completed, to feel

blissful mystery of Him

I find myself in that condition of mind and feelings

When reality gives place to reverie and merges with

The shadowy visions of the first stages of purgatorius ignis

I've carried, on clammy hands, venial sins, to be purged

Of them, being only momentary pain, then soon be on my

Way to Olympus

Here it comes, like a clap of thunder, or like a magic spell

Light one moment and darkness the next—a big fire!

Burning brightly, spreading within me. I scream, "burn me!"

I hear those assembled in the hamlet from whence I have

Come, singing, raising their sacrifices up for my sake--

To be purified.

The Mortal Soul

The long merciless hand when it takes you away
You will part with your house, car, all that you own
All that you have sweated for, gathered day by day
Will now be possessed by relatives once you are gone

You will take nothing with you, not a jewel not a penny
Better then to learn to live without the good things you own
For the soil in its selfish mode won't provide you any
But will let you lie there, empty, naked as you were born

Or, better still, you can try and be dead in Ghana
Where for example if you are a well-known farmer
You can be buried in a coffin the shape of a banana
A driver in a bus, a carpenter in a mallet or a hammer

At least that will make you feel a little worthwhile
You won't regret a bit for having worked so hard

And lost everything at once; your enormous verse file

Will be there, open round you, in case you were a bard

But even those West Africans don't have any luck

For when in the soil you won't identify the colours

The saintly white, the ash grey, or the funeral black

The mortal soul knows only the red on the flowers.

Mosquito

I am in turmoil and no peace in my sleep, little thing
Once in bed, I hate this noise you make over my head
But you do not care and you continue to whine and sing
Moaning as if you already know you will soon be dead

As true as the rising of the sun, I will ensure you are dead
I know your antennae has already caught whiff of my sweat
And you are locating me by my body's odour, heat and breath
You are already planning a skillful land on my forehead

But, little thing, be warned, wisdom belongs to human being
Not to a thin-legged small-winged blood-thirsty insect like you
Do not trust the scanty knowledge you have, oh little thing:
Use of a triple threat of visual, use of olfactory or thermal cue

That is nothing compared to the wisdom of human being
It will only be wise for you to go in for plant nectar or honey

There in that nectar or honey, you can get sugar for survival
And avoid drawing unnecessary duel with a human being

Half asleep, half awake; Bzzz! Something touches my skin
I guess your proboscis has started to pierce my forehead
Slowly, I feel an injection on my flesh, saliva seeping in
Wow! Pain! I startle up -- You swiftly fly away from my bed!

Suddenly, I can hear you flitting back with a fierce grudge
I freeze hands mid-air and I hear you slowly prick my forehead
Pa! Smash! Silence ensures... little thing, you are now sludge
You will never again attempt to suck blood from my head

I quickly slip down from my bed, switches on the room's light
Palms are red -- you are dead -- you will never have another bite
Phew! Nasty bug guts! -- I wash my hands and switch off the light
I can now look forward to having a buzz-free sleep tonight.

Twilight

——*For Grandma*

With a bowed back
A wrinkled face
A grin smile
Half-blind eyes
A toothless mouth

You trundle slowly, grandma
With the support of your walking stick
Into twilight
Owls come your way to sing for you
Cats' purr their dances around you

Nightfall is almost here, grandma
Like a grey shroud
It will cover earth
Soon it will be dark
And we won't see you in the ocean of the night

Bushes will take shapes of ghosts

Rivers sound eerie

The moon be veiled behind dark clouds

You will be lost in the sea of darkness

We won't find you again, grandma.

Golgotha

Head solemnly hanging
As in prayer
Hands widespread
As in an exaggerated hug
Blood-stained
Nail-pierced holes
On the limbs
Disheveled filthy hair
Now hanging down like sisals

Let Pontius Pilate
Bring down the trio
Before the eagles
Come swooping down on the carcasses
The hyenas clank their teeth
The swam of flies
The wafting stench.

The Whole of Life

The whole of life
is trouble
death alone
brings repose

Ephemeral
brief like a rose
today fresh, blossoming
tomorrow it withers

Today a sturdy soul
tomorrow a grieving soul
crumbling
disintegrating

Life's tune enchants the ear
you enjoy the dance

tomorrow

the tune fades away

leaving you

on the floor, sidling

feeling

dry and empty inside

There is nothing

to delight in

the entire journey of life

is trouble.

When the Curtain Falls

When the curtain falls and I the tragic hero exits the stage
Do not shut your eyes and clutch your cheeks in horror
As though I cease to be, as if I have suddenly become an ogre
It will be unnecessary such a dejection and such a wild rage

Just wake up every morn and peek through the bedroom window
There, a reincarnation! - I will be a goat in your animals' pen
Me-e-e-e! I will bleat, smile and express my feelings every morn
Our love will not be lost; it will continue between goat and widow

When the fire is gone, and all that remains is ember and ash
Do not suddenly cringe and turn cold and shiver and grouse
I will be back as a lizard and live on the walls of our house
We shall talk in secret with our love language being hush-hush

I will spread out every day in the morning to warm in the sun
Signal you with my tail and my torso in the sun's rays

These acts will bring to you memory of the good old days
How much we loved, hugged, kissed, and all we had done

When my eyelids close, limbs freeze and my body turn stiff
Do not panic, but tack me in gently, with passion and love
For I will be reborn -- our cow will give birth to me as a calf
And it will utterly be unnecessary for you to mourn and grieve

In the enclosure, I will be couched on my haunches chewing cud
As you scoop dung and mud from the dank floor of the pen
I will be there joyfully smiling and staring at you now and then
Drooling at the mouth as a sign of love, kindness, desire and lust

When twilight catches up with me and I bear a red ribbon
Do not be overwhelmed by condolences from friends
Tell them that it is not in death where everything ends
Then, one day, our hen's egg will crack - there, a chicken is born!

I'll be a hatchling and live in the chicken-run as part of your family

I will chirp and cackle when you throw pellets to me

To tell you that, though gone to the winds, I am back to be

And will always be and that death is only a pathetic fallacy

Don't Cry

If I die, don't cry

Because I would become a rose flower

Grow in your flower garden

And exude fragrance

You will pick me during Christmas

Display me during birthdays

Smell me during wedding ceremonies

I will be part of you

So, if I die, don't cry

If I die, don't be grieved

Because I would become a pumpkin leaf

Grow in your vegetable garden

Pick me for supper in the evenings

Cook me in the kitchen at nights

I will be at the dining table with you

So, if I die, don't be grieved

If I die, don't moan

Because I will become rain

Fall down from the sky

Gather me by the gutters

And wash kitchen utensils with me

I will be in your kitchen

So, if I die, don't moan

If I die, don't scream

Because I will become a tree

Grow in the corner of our homestead

Cut me occasionally for firewood

Keep a heap of me in your kitchen

Make fire and cook *ugali* with me

I will be part of the household

So, if I die, don't scream.

The Slim Path

If you hunger for a home
That lies way beyond the blue
Follow the slim path, its twists and turns
Keep on, though drudgery and irksome

But remember temptation looms here
A fidget could call for a fiasco
Like Lot's wife be a mound of salt
And loose a healing from that intangible largesse hand

You are likely to peek back
And wriggle about in that sludge
That paints earth with grime
And skid down the long slippery way

If you are thirsting for a home
Stifle the dreary weather of your life

Follow the slender, pebbly path

Muddle through as angels do

You will get others there, self-abnegating

Conversing in a peculiar tongue

Babbling abjurations to the unknown

Gasping under fragile crosses

Peer back at the dark hamlet

Where the tenuous path begins

See the muddy world in which you lived

Where nights wrapped you in fey

CHRISTOPHER OKEMWA:
Selected Poems

Chapter

God and the Divinity

When My Body Withers

When my body withers down

And I breathe no more, O Lord

Give me wings to fly

To the mystery of purgatory

And in the purifying waters

Of the sea, O Lord

Let me wash to cleanse my soul

Give me a lesser punishment, O Lord

Not a dismantling of the soul

The severe beating of the body, O Lord

But a gentle slap on the face

A little pinch on the cheek, O Lord

On my way to Olympus

Carry me gently all the way, O Lord

Up the rocky hills of heaven

Down the dark valleys of hell

Let me reach your abode, O Lord

Where eerie silence looms

Where I can rest in your rooms.

On My Way to Olympus

My soul weighs heavy
Upon the conscientious of my being
I step on the tiled porch
With the mind of ungodliness
Let me dip my finger
In the holiness of the stoup
Cross my evil facade
I am on my way to Olympus
Give me a sacrament
Of baptism, of penance
Upon arrival in purgatory
Whip me hard
Give me the bitter cup of purity
To cleanse me of my undoing
And carry me gently
Along the pebbly road
Upon arrival at your holy abode
Rest me in eternal peace.

Seeking for Him

I have solemnly trodden my pathway

Seeking for Him

To touch and to feel His divine texture

More often than not,

I have missed him, finding him embarking

As I arrive

But more so, as it has been,

And in so many ways,

I have often heard him breathe

In the quiet corridors of the wind

His amorphous existence

Embodied in the howling,

Whining, shrilling and shrieking

Of the dark stormy nights

In the frightening burst of

Thunder, poking

His red tongue out in the dark

Clapping, grumbling

And mumbling

Sometimes provoking smoke from

A tree that has caught fire,

A house or a thing

Indicating His anger, fury,

Old men of the village, then,

Slaughter a goat to appease

For sins or evil acts

Committed by the community

Or some individuals involved in the chemistry

Of witchery

You can find Him

In his recreation, in a sea of the sky

Swimming, floating freely

With His one eye open

Without a wink

Relentlessly and consistently

Watching over you in the night

Or, in the morning

Spreading His many fingers over the horizon

And colouring the hill yonder

In an orange paint

His other one eye

Sparkling and eye-squinting

Smiling at you as you open your bedroom window

Or as you tether goats in the fields.

His absence which is also

His invisible presence

Upon a bud

Feel the power of creation

As the petals open as in a lover's embrace

To be a beautiful phenomena of

What He is, or aspire

The contents of His creation to be.

Tufts of the Tall Grass

I have always wanted to know

Where the Maker

Of air and soil lives

Erecting those pillars high up

To hold the firmament in place; in pain

Sobbing Himself out so that we may have rain.

I look up to the sky where

A thick pile of clouds hangs

The blue only glare

Giving little clue.

I walk down to the riverbank.

Fagged out by many centuries

Of creation work, He would be there

Washing the cake of dust

Off His body; the plashes and purls play on

Monotonously, the brown waves

Swirl and churn up

But I don't sight a torso, a toe

Of a man swimming to the shore.

In a splendid fury

I walk through the mystery of the night

So as to bump into Him, vexed

He will retort;

My figure, spectral in a wash

Of moonlight, sight a tall black shadow

Spring forward

Not of the Maker

Not of an angel

But of a desperate mortal in search of truth.

I stop abruptly to listen

To the wind's soft song, picking

Out its notes carefully, one at a time

Feeling the inflection and the varying texture of its tempo

And suddenly -- oyez! His voice

Awesome, yet soothing and caring

Emerge slowly, eerily

Out of the dark green tufts

Of the tall grass.

What I Want Today

Today I want to wake up

Before the sun rises

To praise Him for this new day

Pious, faithful

Attain purification

Cleansing from evil thoughts

Malice, jealousy

Envy and what-not

Throughout this day

I want to carry a smile

On my face, show

Empathy and care

Be kind to a brother

Throw a coin or two

Into a beggar's plate

Speak a word

Of comfort to the elderly

Today, I want to wake up

Before the sun rises.

Someone in Control

In a sleepless night, I open the
Small bed-room window and look out to study
The mystery of the night; a big pool of darkness
Fill the void of the world.
I find it inspiring as well as awesome
The night has a way of making you think there is no life
At all existing anywhere in the world, no God living,
Nothing beyond the black sheet of darkness
And we all might as well be dead.

As I stay blankly staring into this pool of darkness
A star peeps out somewhere up in the sky, then gradually
The moon pops out of the thick rafts of clouds
Like a beautiful bride and rides on across the sky
Smiling down at me by the window.
Suddenly a meteor startlingly shoots down the hillside
Burning a path down the imagined horizon
A sign of existence, of someone in control.

Chapter

Love and Beauty

Your Full Face

Alone in this small single room

I sit watching an empty concrete wall

I try to count

The number of stones

That went into its construction

Try to imagine the name of the painter

Who made the walls shine

His family background

His level of education

How he twisted his wrinkled face

To make strokes with his brush

How he bit his lower lip

In pushing the brush up the wall

The pose he took

To reach crannies and nooks of the house

At times, unconsciously, I shake my head

To the unknown distant music

Either of a bird, or of

A band, or of an old

Tune coming back from the past

Or, it could simply, or perhaps, be fiction characters

Who beat drums in my head

Or, at times, unconsciously, I clench my teeth

To a distant barking of a dog

Imagining it is biting a child

My six-year old daughter

Frightened, I scream and grief

Condemn and curse

At times, I close my eyes

And let my mind wander back to Kenya

To our children at School

To our house

To the balcony teeming with old shoes

Slippers, tattered clothes

To the litter bin at the veranda

The bees that buzz at the portico

To the noise from the neighbour's house

But the larger part of the day

I spend looking out of the latticed window

During which time I see

A clump of short trees in the fields

With their massive quivering foliage

Dew dripping from the grey boughs

The unseen wind whizzing through them

Then, slowly, gradually

Your green short dress,

With black embroidery

And strips of blue

Appears, then by and by

Your eyes, your lips

Then your full pretty face.

(Selected from *Love from Afro-Catalonia*, 2020)

I Love You Not As...

I love you not as one can love a bar of chocolate

Or a mango juice or a banana fruit or a mushroom

Or as one can love roasted groundnuts in a plate

I love you as one can love an exotic dream

In which the dreamer is in a wedding costume

And his bride is fair of face and is in full bloom

I love you not as one can love a moon-lit sky

Or a tall tree, or a blue sea or a star in the night

Or as one can love a grasshopper, a termite or a butterfly

I love you as one can love a red ray of sunlight

When the morning, like ripe tomato, bursts in the horizon

And the foot-steps of the last night are long gone

I love you not as one can love a song of a bird in the nest

Or the whizzing of a wind or the buzzing of a bee that flits

Or as one can love the whistling of a tree in the forest

I love you as one can love the sound of ghosts and spirits

Who live in the waters of the sea or dwells in the cemetery

And is heard rising and falling at night in a puzzle of mystery

I love you not as one can love the aroma of fresh coffee

Or the smell of raw soil or rotten leaves dumped in a pit

Or as one can love the fragrance of a rose or a lilac tree

I love you as one can love the smell of a lover's armpit

The erotic texture and the feel of its bushy hair

The moist and its rivulets of sweat when she is bare

I love you not as one can love a genius work of art

Or a sight of a magnificent city sprawled in the sun

Or as one can love a new pair of shoes, shorts or shirt

I love you as one can love an old tattered photo

In which one is a child playing in a puddle of mud

With an aura of innocence, honesty and Godliness

This Morning

This morning I woke up

With a sense of loss

I found silence holding the four corners of my room

And a mystery

A sort of Muse

Playing in the light and in the darkness

Between the walls and empty spaces

I slipped down from my narrow bed

Quickly ransacked my suitcase for your photos

I couldn't find any

Scrolled down the screen of my phone

With nervous fingers

I didn't see one -- my cheeks flashed white

Looking at the mirror on the wall

A bubbly curve formed at the corner of my mouth

My forehead became bright just like a sunny day

The evidence of desire

For a loved one back home

Now seated at the table

I sketch your body on a piece of paper

An imagination of the woman that I love

An expression within me

Of whom I know you have been to me

I pencil your thick lips, whiten your

Teeth, circle twin mounds on your chest

Dots your deep sensuous navel

I repeatedly scratch on the pupils of your eyes

Making them dilated, adds more pencil

On the cheeks to make them dazzling and bewitching

Shades the hair to make it glossy

Cleaves your forehead with two wrinkles

(You can't be young forever)

Gives a dark shade to your nose

A light colour to your chin

Then the neck of a swan to stabilize your head

I sit back to examine the finished work

My body twitches

I move my lips down

To kiss it

Suddenly I hear a loud sigh from a distance

A silent longing

A lusty act from a lover

With the utterance "l miss you, oh my dear love"

(Selected from *Love from Afro Catalonia*, 2020, Kistrech Theatre International)

Watching Her

I watch her

Sprawl her body on a white sheet

She is an endless blue sea

Studded with dots of stars

Gorgeous

Delicious

Her lips and mine

Seek for a spot

Somewhere in the crescent moon

To lock into each other

The light fades

Our hearts knot and entangle

In the middle

Of our dreamy world.

I Am Soon Coming Back Home

I am alone in Olot, I no longer want to be alone
I want to come home very soon, my dear love
I want to meet with you, to kiss you, to love you
To reach for your lips, your tongue and your teeth

I want to meet with you soon, my dearest love
I miss you and want to connect with you again
To meet with you, to reach out to your breath
Your scent, your aroma, your sweat and your odour

I have suffered loneliness, longing, wishes and desire
I want to come home to you and for you, my dear love
To sit at the balcony and watch the heavens at night
And count with you the stars in the bowl of the sky

I want to come home very soon, my precious love
Once more, as we have always done in the past

Walk to the fields together in the grey evenings
Catch the termites, the butterflies and the grasshoppers

I don't want to stay in Olot any longer, my dear love
I want to come home to see the evening rains
Enjoy once more the tapping music on the roof
And the muddy puddle that forms outside our house

I really want to come home, my dearest love
To see your hair, your face, your neck, your chest
To see your skirt, your blouse and your belt
To see your lingerie, your bra and your pajama

I miss you and love you and want to be with you
I want to listen to your voice as it always came to me
I want to listen to your giggles and your laughter
Hear how you belch, sneeze, click, sniff and snore

I want to come home and walk with you to the fields
And listen to the birds' songs from their nests
Then hear you sing to me as we walk in the woods
Holding hands, embracing, hugging and kissing

We shall catch fireflies in the dark night together
And treat it as an act of romance and love
Keep them in a small basket as we have always done
And watch them flash their lights like your twinkling eyes

Each day I imagine departing from Olot in Spain
Leaving behind this room, this dreary weather
Freezing pools, cold roads and snowy mountains
And come home to sunshine and warm soft rains

I Get Fascinated

I get fascinated
With the curve
Around your hips
The depth
Of the
Naval
The roundness
Of your
Belly
The gentle descent
Down the fields
Of bushes
Of woods
To the
Spring
Of joy
Stream
Of excitement

My Wife at 40

The bloom

has come off

the rose

rather quickly

panicky

demanding

40 lights a fuse under you

psychotic tara-tara-tara acts

nervous

irrational behavior

the fuse effect

life's mire

humbled to wade through it.

You Wear It Like A Chain You Wear Around Your Neck

The war has just begun within you

Oh lovely one

Its output can easily be traced

In the fat around your abdomen

The tenderness of your breasts

I can measure its severity

In the depression and anxiety on your face

The low mood

Irritable reactions

And the crying spells.

Your pain seethes through my veins

I become weary

I sweat at night as you do

Grope along the walls at night

To the toilet

To frequently urinate with you

It is a new norm for you,

It is a new norm for me

I seem to understand you well

I wear your shoe, too often

And I know the pain therein

Atrophic vaginitis

You wear it like a chain you wear around the neck

It is a path all women tread

That interior wanting

Is carried away by the wind of undesire

Dyspareunia

thin labia

the painful pathway

anxiety

It is a dark path both of us walk on.

Stain of Red Moods

take a peek

into your panties

to see

the stain of red moods

that has painted the canvas

of your being

with stains of seven winds

on whose wings

ride the demons that has bolted

out of you.

They blow us off like dry leaves of a tree

The red-coloured tantrums

The anger

The tumultuous

The turbulence.

In Your Own Centre

In your own centre

You are a loser

Clinging onto those tendrils

as though the world

is sliding down on the secret portion of their leaves

The birds sing of your

Unclasped heroism

You are a broken wing of an angel who is flying

At half mast

You are gone, just for now

I wonder what you will become tomorrow:

A wren that builds a nest

While the eclipse shuts out the sun?

Or, a weaverbird that has mastered the seasons

To beak bits of its dreams into her nestlings?

Let me carry you to the clouds

On which life depends so much for its beauty of mystery

So that you decorate the sky, air and wind

With pieces of your leaking dreams

At least now you have become

A high priest, a hermaphrodite

Who manufactures rain drops

A blessing to the next generation

But straddles your sacred twin body

Upon two familiar but separate worlds.

To Damiana

If sex makes me happy, kindly give me
Don't skimp as you do with porridge and rice
Let me fall through slowly and beauty see
Make you sigh and smile as I start to rise
If sex excites me, allow me come in
Through your gate of pearls, silver and gold
To reach a joy never before seen
And learn to tell a tale never been told
If I do love sex, kindly love it, too
Support me to sail on and find a place
Where treasure of fire is lit for two
To heat both our souls and put them ablaze
Therefore, let us swim and reach the sea-bed
Sing songs while the sea swirls slimy and red

If I insist having it, be kind, dear
Don't wear a wrinkle on your pretty face

Or indicate dislike by showing some fear

Try the animus in your eyes to erase

Therefore, dear, allow me to the sea board

Finger the sea grass, tickle the sea kale

The sea-lion extending its hot cord

See it turn sea-worthy, the swollen male

Kindly, dear, let us have a seamless flow

Whittle down sea-weed along the seaway

The sailing ship to burning sea-bed go

My world this way and that way keep its sway

As I lay intact in this distant sea-bed

Crumpling on sea-side---kindly hold my head!

Leaving Home

When I left home this morning
We stood at the gate
Like two strangers, in an awful moment

Staring at each other
Your nails were varnished
A brilliant shade of red

A pink cow-girl outfit you wore
Made your face narrow and pinched
Your large, heavy-lidded eyes

Even-sized white teeth, rumpled hair
That stood like sisal on your head--
Gave you an unshaven charm of youth

I remember the cat came out
To make few burrows between our legs
You moved closer, your hands

A swathe of wool and fur around me
We kissed; you fumbled for words
While tears came down like burning rain

I felt the wet warmth on my chest
Take care while in Colombia, you said
In the shrill, little-girl tone.

A Sudden Rush of Love

I woke up with a sense of loss

And found a gentle pool of silence

Holding the four corners of my bedroom

I looked up and saw her face there

Staring down from the wall photographs

Our eyes caught and entangled

And stars came into my vision

I felt a sudden rush of love

Rise up from the warm bed-sheets

Spilling softly into my heart

Pushing itself up through my eyes

Filling the whole of my brain

Then slowly assembled itself together

Spilling out into gentle streams

Of soft smiles and erotic sighs
And boiled down into the sheets
From whence it had come.

Let Me Know

If I ever offended you

Discuss it with me, dear love

Don't keep it in the heart for too long

Let me know of the mistake

I have made, dear love

That makes you pale, mute

If I once shouted at you

And you were flustered, dear love

It is because I cared, or so I thought

Let us talk with open minds

Of the flaws, the pitfalls

And mend the broken fences

Bring to an end this silence

And hear your voice again, dear love

As it always came to me.

Your Arrivals

When I hear the gate creaking

The banging, grass rustling along

The footpath towards the piazza, an abrupt

Silence, then, slowly, the key turning the door-hole

I simply know it is your arrival

But in most cases

It has simply been an illusion

The wind on passing might want to rustle

The grass, or a lizard accidentally falls

On the concrete porch, turns over and stampedes

Across the path, sounding like someone going back in a hurry

Hey! I call, only to be answered

By the empty echo in the room

I have had those numerous arrivals

Your arrivals

And those echoes, too, that wash

Upon me like elusive dreams

And have had my feelings falsely elated.

Nascent

There is something, nascent
That has begun
To pick up its gradient

In its climbing
It touches the loft of the mind
Sprinkling about its aroma

When I tilt the frame of my mind
It bounces against its walls
Scattering my thoughts around

Dazzling! -I love it
It fills the heart with glamour
And charm

It continuous to jell

Graceful and sweet

Of overwhelming oomph.

CHRISTOPHER OKEMWA:
Selected Poems

Chapter

Coming out of Isolation

7

It Is Curfew Time !

the curfew time has come

Oh, hurry up -- faster!

police position themselves

in street corners

Ready to strike

Women hurriedly fold their wares

And rush to the storehouse

Children scream behind their mothers' backs

As people run home from the market

The curfew time is here!

Matatus zoom past

hooting and beeping

Music speakers blare up

I say a hip! A hap! A hip to the hippie!

Don't stop to rap to the bang boogie!

I rap to the beat nobody can rap!

those inside hold their heads in their palms

shut their eyes in pain

and curse the driver.

a pedestrian runs across the road carelessly

nearly being hit by the speeding motorists

street boys take advantage of the hustle and bustle:

struggle

scratch

maim

snatch

a bag, a watch, a mobile phone

disappear behind tall buildings

into dark narrow alleys

It is curfew time!

Boda boda

Pick two passengers at a time

Three at once

Four at ago

Swoops down the road

Like an eagle

Beeping

Hollering

Snaking through the snarl-up

Driving on the sidewalk

Give way! Move! Give way! Move!

The mad man will shout

Sending pedestrians scampering for their lives

It is curfew time!

Shop-doors creak

and bang

grille shutters roll down

and hit the horizontal concrete base

with a thud

owners rush out

swinging bags on their shoulders

quickly enter their cars and zoom off

dust rises up in the distant hill

the sky's blue dome turns brown

it is curfew time!

An old man is seen

Quickly-quickly, trudging home

Supporting himself with a walking stick

His mouth rapidly opens and shuts

Mumbling to himself

kurona! Kurona! Oh kurona!

He curses and condemns

He shakes his head

Fury and pain wrinkle his forehead

It is curfew time!

Yu-wi-iiii, yu-wi-iii, yu-wi-iiii
Police siren cuts the air
Wailing, like those old women in a corona funeral
People scramble
Road barricaded
Distortion, bribery, fine, jail-term
A huge snarl-up
Horn-honking!
Horn-beeping!
Cursing! Condemning!
Corona misery eats deep
Eh! It is curfew time!

(Published in *Between the Walls and Empty Spaces*, Demer Press,
Netherlands, 2022)

What Colour?

What colour can I paint

your name, oh corona?

In white like

a frozen snow?

or in red like blood?

What if I paint your name

in black

like a shroud?

or brown like a casket?

Let me paint the name

in grey

like the pyre

or blue

like a sad sea.

Most probably

I could paint your name in soil-brown colour

like a sepulchre

with streaks of grey

on your delicate back and arms

like a dull cloud.

The Garbage Heap

Every day I drive past here

I open the window

To allow the stench

Waft in with ease

To test whether

My sense of smell is still intact

And that I have not become positive.

If I don't catch the smell

That waft from the garbage heap

Then I will know I have been

Caught up

With the tiny microbe

And I have no escape

Except through the window

Of prayer and immunity.

So I keep sticking out my nose

Through the window

And breathing in the stench

To keep myself afloat.

A Harbinger of Good Things to Come

The world is no longer quivering

Heaving

Running over itself

Like a child in fright, hollering

Screaming to get away from a stranger

There is noticeable calm

The red smudge of blood

On the celestial cosmic

Is washing down by divine rain

The frightening breath

Afloat in the cosmic

Is swept away into

The peaceful corridors of the wind

Desperately whining

Whistling, condemning

The one present, who

Is also a mysterious absence

Sentinel in the celestial cosmic

Drops stars down to us, like confetti from the heavens

We stretch our clammy palms

In supplication and in abeyance

Tend for me, oh Engoro

Tend for me, oh, Engoro

And the sound with which the cluster falls

On our hands is soothing

And the humming sound

Of the smouldering rain

The gentle thunderstorms

Brilliant lightening, chirps of crickets

Tend to blend the sound of gurgling waters of the river

And the conversing forest trees

Seem to whisper to the twittering of birds

There is peace and harmony

Fulfillment and life in abundance

-A harbinger of good things to come.

I Came to Nairobi

I came to Nairobi this morning

To see Corona

I hear it walks on the streets

In stilettos

Wears a hood

Like a burglar

Wears a mask askew

Like a teenage boy

It barks about like a rabid toothless dog

Its tail, with a sting at the tip

Wags away between its legs

Its eyelids purse together

downcast

Shy, timid

Like a village boy of 12 years

Who is being driven to face the circumciser's knife

A ceremony he abhors

But has to undergo altogether

Like a famous boxer

Who goes to the ring with a past injury

Yet his supporters yell

With a deafening applause

I came to the city this morning

Disturbed with curiosity

To see corona

I hear it runs on the streets

With a shocking speed

When it hears a slight noise

It stops, its steps falter on the sidewalk

And falls over itself many times,

Squeaking like a squirrel

It looks at people as though wishing it could live on earth

Most of the time

It flies to thin air

Leaving its liquid shadow on the pavement.

Bending Down to Pick Up Its Old Cloth

The terror and the fear

The alarm

Is fading fast

Diminishing, gone or about to go

The lethal claws of the microbe

Is no longer dreadful

The gentle footsteps

Of the divine messenger

The Guardian spirit

Is heard yonder

Blooming flowers grow in our minds

We catch with our eyes

Soft images of sunlight

Glimpse into the moon-lit nights

Gently-burning candles

Listen to the soft twitters of birds

It is morning

The night has disintegrated like pieces of chalk

The dawn is gone

Or about to go

People are starting to gather on the streets

Hugging and kissing

Mask-less faces display laughter and giggles

Life has come back, or is soon coming back

In abundance

Rushing in, bending down to pick up its old cloth.

Coming Out of Isolation

Don't tire, or breathe in
the air of desperation
or dark pessimism
a season of fear
is now behind us
spring is yonder
new fresh buds of hope
are beginning to grow
in the core of our being
a new fire has sprung up
the sunlight
is bright upon the hills
the birds are able to sing again
fields are spread with fresh grass
the earth is back to life
the hugging
the kissing

the partying

a new beginning

a season of spring.

(First published in *Spring's Blue Ribbon: International Poems*, Edited by Gino Leineweber, VerlagExpeditionen, 2021)

語言文學類　PG2999　秀詩人118

蜂蜜酒上的暮光：
漢英雙語詩集

作　　　者／克里斯托夫·歐克姆瓦（Christopher Okemwa）
譯　　　者／羅得彰（Te-chang Mike Lo）
責任編輯／邱意珺
圖文排版／黃莉珊
封面設計／魏振庭

發 行 人／宋政坤
法律顧問／毛國樑　律師
出版發行／秀威資訊科技股份有限公司
　　　　　114台北市內湖區瑞光路76巷65號1樓
　　　　　電話：+886-2-2796-3638　傳真：+886-2-2796-1377
　　　　　http://www.showwe.com.tw
劃撥帳號／19563868　戶名：秀威資訊科技股份有限公司
　　　　　讀者服務信箱：service@showwe.com.tw
展售門市／國家書店（松江門市）
　　　　　104台北市中山區松江路209號1樓
　　　　　電話：+886-2-2518-0207　傳真：+886-2-2518-0778
網路訂購／秀威網路書店：https://store.showwe.tw
　　　　　國家網路書店：https://www.govbooks.com.tw

2023年11月　BOD一版
定價：350元
版權所有　翻印必究
本書如有缺頁、破損或裝訂錯誤，請寄回更換

讀者回函卡

國家圖書館出版品預行編目

蜂蜜酒上的暮光：漢英雙語詩集 / 克里斯托夫.歐
　克姆瓦 (Christopher Okemwa) 著 ; 羅得彰 (Te-
　chang Mike Lo) 譯. -- 一版. -- 臺北市 : 秀威資
　訊科技股份有限公司, 2023.11
　　　面 ；　　公分. -- (語言文學類 ; PG2999) (秀詩
　人 ; 118)
　中英對照
　BOD版
　譯自 : Christopher Okemwa : selected poems.
　ISBN 978-626-7346-27-3 (平裝)

886.5651　　　　　　　　　　　　112015791